Wild Rose Summer

Brides of Cedar Falls, Book #5

Jo Grafford, writing as Jovie Grace

SECOND EDITION: This book was originally part of the Christmas Rescue Series. It has since been rewritten and expanded to be part of the **Brides of Cedar Falls Series** — uplifting historical romance full of faith, hope, love, and cowboys!

ISBN: 978-1-63907-074-9

Chapter 1: New Beginnings
Rose

June, 1868

Rose Marie Addington clutched her travel bag against her chest as the wagon bumped along the hard-packed trail. The bag contained everything she owned — her late mother's opal wedding ring, her late father's pen, and his last partially used bottle of ink. The bag also carried both copies of her current manuscript, the original one and the new one she was painstakingly recopying. Between the two, she possessed more than four hundred pages of a haunting love story, with countless phrases crossed out and the revised words scrawled above or below them.

Though her story, *A Mountain Tryst*, might never be set in type or receive a proper leather binding, she'd gone ahead and signed it as *R. Addington*. She'd shortened her first name to a single letter, knowing the unlikely chance of ever being published might become a little less unlikely if the printer were to assume she was a man.

Hugging her travel bag more tightly against the front

of her faded blue calico dress, she squinted through the evening sunlight to survey the jagged foothills of the distant mountains. All publishing woes aside, she was on a rather exciting adventure of her own today. She was on her way to a small town in Texas named Cedar Falls, where she'd been invited to live with an aunt she'd never met — a wealthy spinster who resided in a large adobe mansion with a whole platoon of servants, according to her letters.

Rose was still piecing together the details of why she was just now finding out she had an elderly aunt as rich as royalty. In one of her letters, Aunt Winifred Monroe had attempted to explain the highlights of the mystery. Apparently, Rose's mother had married a poor railway worker for love and had been summarily disinherited by their parents. Afterward, her mother's older sister, Winifred, had inherited the western spur of the Monroes' vast shipping company. Their brother, Jack, had inherited the southern spur, which had been largely destroyed during the war. Until the war had broken out, her Uncle Jack and his four children had been living only a few miles away from Rose on the posher side of Atlanta.

After being led to believe she had no family left in the world, it was a real head-scratcher to discover she had a spinster aunt, a widower uncle, and four cousins. *Four of them!*

What Aunt Winifred hadn't yet explained to Rose's satisfaction was why Rose's mother had been so thoroughly written out of the Monroe family's lives. It was equally puzzling why Rose was being written back in.

She was more grateful, though, than any words she could spin from her creative author mind. It felt like a miracle that Aunt Winifred had come to the magnanimous decision to invest some of her fortune towards the launch of her impoverished youngest niece into society.

From what Rose could gather, her aunt's knees had been crippled from birth and were growing worse by the day. Despite her deteriorating condition, she'd gone to the tremendous effort of employing multiple detectives to track down Rose. And now that she'd succeeded, she was bringing the only offspring of her wayward middle sibling back into the family fold.

Rose would be serving as Aunt Winifred's personal secretary and companion of sorts now that her cousin, Anna Kate, had married and was no longer in the position to fill the role full time. Rose would be juggling her new responsibilities around a rather rigorous-sounding set of daily lessons in singing, dancing, painting, and needlework. If she understood her aunt's intentions correctly, she was to be paraded before every eligible bachelor in town before the summer's end. Some young women in her shoes might be offended by such highhandedness.

All Rose felt, however, was gratitude. Her sudden change in fortune was still sinking in, but her shoulders already felt a thousand pounds lighter. She wouldn't miss the drudgery of the poorhouse where she'd lived and worked for the past eleven months — not one bit! If marrying a man she barely knew was her ticket to avoiding a repeat of such hardships, then that was exactly what she planned to do. She'd written enough stories about true love to understand it was all they were. Stories. In real life, a person needed food in their belly and a roof over their head to stay alive. Her own mother — may she rest in peace — was proof enough that a body couldn't survive on love alone.

"You doin' alright over there?" Her driver pushed back

his well-worn Stetson and cast a worried sideways glance across the bench they were sharing. She was his only passenger. Her aunt had sent him to pick her up from the train depot. He'd been pretty quiet up until now.

"I am, sir. Thank you." A trickle of dampness on her left cheek made her frown. She brushed at it with her fingertips. That was odd! "I didn't realize it was raining." She glanced up at the clear evening sky. Pink and orange streaks were fingering their way across the horizon, signaling the start of sunset.

"It ain't, ma'am," the white-bearded fellow informed her gently. He dug in the pocket of his patched denim overalls and produced a wrinkled handkerchief. "There, there," he clucked, holding it out to her.

She stared at his handkerchief in puzzlement.

"Take it, miss," he urged. "It's clean."

Another few seconds ticked past before she realized what he was talking about. He must have assumed she was weeping. She brushed her fingertips across her cheeks again and discovered more moisture there. *Good gracious!* She *was* weeping. *Why am I weeping?* Surely, they were happy tears. So many good things were happening so quickly to her. Perhaps she was simply a little overwhelmed by it all.

"Thank you, sir," she murmured, accepting the crumpled square of fabric. Sniffling a few times, she dabbed her face dry with a corner of it. As he'd promised, it was clean.

"Where do you hail from?" He adopted a companionable tone, as if he wasn't sitting next to a woman who was acting like a watering pot for no good reason.

"From Atlanta, sir."

"Just like Miss Monroe's other niece." He harrumphed loudly. "It's no wonder you have the sound of magnolias and pecan pie in your voice." He pronounced the word *pecan*

4

like *pea-can.* "And you're more than welcome to drop all that *sir* business. Most folks call me Jensen. I run the livery. Or used to. My son, Ed, runs it now. I just help out now and then."

It was impossible not to smile at his open-faced friendliness. "Pleased to meet you, Jensen. I'm Rose Addington."

His head jerked back in her direction. "Addington, you say?"

"Yes, sir. Why do you ask?"

"I thought you looked familiar." He gave her another long, searching look. "You must be related to that poor fella who hitchhiked his way into town some thirty-odd years ago and married, er..." He lapsed into awkward silence.

"My mother," Rose supplied with a watery smile. Apparently, her late mother's disinherited state was no secret to the local townsfolk. Her curiosity about the Monroe family notched up a few more degrees, along with her level of uneasiness about them. Perhaps she'd been a little hasty in assuming her latest adventure was going to have a happy ending. Not that it would've changed her decision to accept her aunt's unexpected invitation to travel west. Rose had been caught between the proverbial rock and a hard place when her Aunt Winifred's first letter had found its way into her hands.

"Well, I'll be!" Jensen looked as pleased as all get out that he'd correctly identified her. "And now you've come to live with your uppity aunt on the fancy side of town."

At her wide-eyed look of astonishment, he hastened to apologize. "Beggin' your pardon, miss." He sheepishly ducked his head. "I s'pose that wasn't the most mannerly description of the woman who owns half our town."

Rose smiled warily at his description, half tempted to pinch herself to make sure she wasn't dreaming. "I've never met my aunt, though I'm very anxious to do so. Is she truly all that...uppity?" The thought tickled her funny bone. Wasn't the starchy creature going to be surprised when her niece from the poorhouse arrived with nothing more than the clothes on her back?

"I, er..."

When Jensen refused to meet her gaze, Rose burst out laughing. "Uppity was putting it mildly, eh? You have me picturing a veritable ogre, sirrah!"

He looked aghast. "I would never say such a thing about a lady, ma'am."

You didn't have to. "Tell me more about her," Rose coaxed, swiveling in his direction. She'd been practically dying of curiosity about the woman throughout her entire journey west. "We have plenty of time to burn."

"A few miles." His voice was cautious. "That should give us twenty minutes or so to jaw."

"Wonderful!" Her smile widened. "I'm anxious to hear everything you can tell me about my aunt and the town she lives in. And, by all means, speak your mind, if that's what has you looking so worried. There's no need to sugarcoat anything on my behalf." She hadn't been raised with sugarcoating. She preferred honesty.

"We-e-ell." Jensen drew the word out as if unsure how to describe the woman whose doorstep he would soon deposit her on.

Impatience welled in Rose. Surely, her driver didn't expect her to spend what little time they had left together doing no more than listening to him hemming and hawing! "I already know she's quite a bit older than my mother was and crippled, to boot."

"That she is, miss. She used to walk with a cane."

Jensen announced that nugget of information like it was no big deal. "Lately, though, she's been bound to a wheelchair."

"I'm very sorry to hear it." Rose could only imagine how out of sorts that would put a person. Perhaps being crippled was the real reason for the crotchetiness that Jensen had alluded to.

"Make no mistake." Jensen gave her another searching look. "She doesn't complain much about it." He sniffed. "I reckon she's too busy barking orders like a general to everyone around her."

The vision of an ogre inside Rose's head transitioned to an imperious queen — one with a golden crown tipped sideways as she leaned forward in her wheelchair, bellowing royal decrees to her lowly subjects.

"Does she have any friends?" Rose was fascinated by everything she'd heard so far about her aging aunt. And more than a little puzzled. Jensen was being a bit stingy on the details.

"Lots of 'em, miss." He made a face that she couldn't quite define. "When you have as much money in the bank as Miss Winifred Monroe, everyone's your friend."

"Oh?" Rose wasn't sure if his last statement was intended as a compliment or yet more criticism.

"She has hired help she can trust. A driver named Rupert who takes her everywhere she wants to go." His expression brightened. "They've been working together for so long, he's more like kin than an employee."

Rose's image of her aunt shimmered back into one of ordinary flesh and blood. "Who else works for my aunt?"

"A whole army of servants." Jensen scratched the back of his neck. "She's got a cook and a butler."

"My aunt has a butler?" Rose's jaw dropped. She'd

known her aunt was wealthy, but a butler sounded...well, extravagant.

"That would be Rupert again." Jensen's eyes twinkled merrily. "He's her right-hand man. Plus, she's got a pair of gardeners, a bevy of housemaids, and some ranch hands. Not sure how many." He shook his grizzled head, grinning to himself. He was clearly enjoying his tale.

"That's a lot of servants." Her aunt certainly hadn't exaggerated the size of her household staff in her letters.

"That it is." Jensen bobbed his chin up and down. "She hired a new man of business not too long ago. Her last one retired. I dunno his name, but someone said he might be a distant relation. We don't see much of him, since he travels most of the time."

Yet another family member? Rose grabbed hungrily onto that piece of information. *If only I could be so fortunate!* A few weeks ago, she'd believed herself to be the last of her family. For reasons she didn't yet understand, and might never understand, her late parents hadn't so much as hinted about the existence of other relatives. Their silence on the topic was making less and less sense the closer she drew to Cedar Falls.

She pressed a hand to her heart, unsure why it was thumping so hard. Drawing a deep breath, she let it out slowly.

Silence settled between her and Jensen as the sun descended on the horizon. The beauty of the craggy blue and brown ridges rising in front of them constricted Rose's throat. It was as if Jensen was driving her straight into one of the stories she'd penned.

Writing was her secret hobby. She'd been scribbling in private for as long as she could remember. Her father, Jonas Addington, had caught her composing one of her earliest short stories by the light of a lantern one evening. Instead of reprimanding her for her foolishness, he'd encouraged her to drop everything and start writing each time the inspiration struck. He'd been her biggest fan, bragging that he would be related to a famous author someday. Though it might still be true, he hadn't lived to see it.

Rose lost track of the time as she drifted through bitter-sweet nostalgia. The orange sun ripened to a ball of crimson, spreading even more marvelous slashes of color across the sky. Shades of red bled into shades of purple. The ground between her and the mountains became dotted with tumbleweed and cacti. Tall, dry grasses waved as far as she could see in the opposite direction. She didn't exactly doze off, but she drifted in a haze of nervous anticipation.

"We're getting close," Jensen offered after a stretch of silence. "No more'n a handful of minutes left, I'd say."

Rose sat up and arched her back to work out a kink. "That means it'll still be daylight when we arrive. I can't wait to see everything!" *My new home.*

"Can't blame you for that." Jensen leaned forward to nicker at his team of horses. They picked up their pace a little. "I'd be excited, too, if I was going to live in a castle."

The roof lines of Cedar Falls wavered in the distance and took shape as they continued to roll in its direction. Soon, Rose could make out the spires of a church.

Jensen waved a gnarled hand. "There's the church and the new Pine Street Cafe up ahead. If you're ever looking for a decent spot to eat, Felipe knows how to turn a steak, and his cousin can whip up an apple pie like you wouldn't believe."

"It sounds delicious." Rose's stomach growled, making her squirm uncomfortably on the hard wooden bench. *Mercy!* It had been way too many hours since her last meal.

9

Due to her scarcity of funds, she'd limited herself to one meal per day on the long train ride west. Since her wallet had run dry, she was thankful she would be arriving at her destination shortly.

They crossed a wooden bridge that was arched over a dry creek bed.

"The town square's over there." Jensen angled his chin toward the center of town. "It's smack dab in the middle of Main Street where we're headed."

As the evening shadows deepened, lamps and lanterns flickered to life inside the boarding house windows on Main Street. Most of the other businesses looked like they were already closed, including one with a sign designating it as Town Hall and a tidy looking wooden storefront marked Post Office. Cedar Falls wasn't nearly as big and bustling as Atlanta, but the buildings and streets looked tidy and in good repair. The stalwart evergreens dotting both sides of the street were downright charming.

Jensen nosed his team of horses in an easterly direction. "There's the livery." He motioned toward a set of stables. "And the blacksmith." It was located a few doors down from the livery. "And the gunsmith's shop across the way." He gave a low whistle. "The young feller who owns it just received a shipment of Colts." He shook his head in admiration. "Double-action revolvers. The first I've ever seen of those. I need to git myself down there and purchase one 'afore he sells plumb out!"

Right. Rose sniffed. She'd all but forgotten this was the wild west. Her mother had witheringly described it as a place where every male twirled a pair of six-shooters.

"What?" Jensen lifted one bushy gray brow at her. "You don't shoot?"

"Of course not!" She couldn't think of anything more

distasteful. "What need would a lady have for a gun?" That is, assuming a young woman in a tattered dress had a right to call herself that in this part of the country.

He looked at her like she was crazy. "For hunting your dinner if you don't have a whole brigade of servants to do it for you. For defending yourself, should the need ever arise."

"I see." Rose wrinkled her nose, not really comprehending at all. Even while living at the poorhouse, her food had come from either the mercantile or the chicken yard behind the boarding house. She'd just as soon let someone else aim between the eyes of the beef and the venison she consumed. She hid a shudder of revulsion. Guns were something she most definitely didn't aspire to own. Not now. Not ever!

The horses clip-clopped past the livery. As Jensen had promised, a few doors down was the gunsmith shop. A tall man was lounging comfortably against the front porch railing, with one boot propped on the lowest rung. He raised a hand to them as his admiring gaze swept over her.

"Hiya, there, Lancaster!" Her driver called cheerfully, tipping the brim of his hat.

"Evening, Jensen!" The man shot him a two-fingered salute, though he didn't spare the old liveryman so much as a glance. He was too busy assessing Rose.

Lancaster. Rose was utterly fascinated by the man's name. It sounded like a hero in a fairytale, the kind who rode off into the sunset to battle dragons and other foul beasts. She wondered what the man's surname was and if it was of equal literary worthiness.

He was young and well dressed — not too many years older than her own twenty years, if she was an accurate judge of age. The upper half of his face was shaded by the brim of a brown Stetson, and he wore a pale blue dress shirt beneath a leather vest. Short-clipped brown sideburns merged with an equally short-clipped brown beard that did nothing to hide the curl of his upper lip.

They were too far away in the wagon for her to determine the exact color of his eyes. All she knew was that they were something dark and rich, infused with male intensity. She experienced the sudden longing for Jensen to stop and issue a proper introduction. Unfortunately, he kept his wagon wheels turning down the hard-packed dirt of Main Street.

Wanting to at least acknowledge the gunsmith, Rose smiled shyly and fluttered her fingers at him.

He nodded to acknowledge her greeting, though he didn't wave back.

A shiver worked its way up her spine. Not a shiver of fear, per se, more like one of excitement. Or anticipation. According to her aunt's letters, her life was about to undergo a metamorphosis. In Winifred Monroe's own words, she planned to give her long-lost niece a coat of social polish that would have her married off by summer's end.

It was inevitable that Rose's thoughts drifted to Lancaster's married state. Or lack thereof. Not that her oh-so-proper aunt would approve of her courting a gunsmith any more than the Monroes had approved of Rose's mother courting a railway worker.

"What is your gunsmith's name again?" She turned her head sideways to continue observing the man from beneath her lashes. "You drove past so quickly, I didn't quite catch all of it."

"My apologies, ma'am." Jensen waved a hand toward the gunsmith's shop that was fast fading into the distance. "That was ol' Lancaster Tracy back there."

Tracy. She repeated the surname dreamily inside her head. It most definitely had the ring of a hero to it. A wild west kind of hero. She ignored the warnings her mother had left ringing in her ears and allowed her imagination to drift to more pleasant territory.

"Don't know him real well, since he arrived in town recently. He seems like a decent fellow, though. Came from somewhere back east, I believe, and worked his way west as a bounty hunter. Sure learned a thing or two about guns along the way. We're mighty glad a man of his caliber decided to set up shop here in Cedar Falls. No pun intended."

"A bounty hunter," Rose sighed. If that wasn't a modern-day dragon slayer, she didn't know what was.

Jensen shot her a puzzled look. "Well, here we are, miss. Your new home."

Rose had been so busy daydreaming up a medieval version of Lancaster Tracy in shining armor that she'd not paid much attention to what was rising in front of them.

"Oh, my!" She gulped. Though it wasn't the stately Old World mansion she'd pictured inside her head, the ranch home was every bit as massive as a fortress. It was half hidden by the forest of cedar trees the town had been named after. A wide veranda spanned the white adobe front of the home, and dormer windows with balconies graced the second story. A lengthy addition on each side of the house had transformed the structure into a giant U shape.

"You sure got the *oh my* part right." Jensen started to hop down from the driver's seat, but Rose stopped him by placing a hand on his arm. He'd seen younger days, and he looked tired. Unaccustomed to being waited on hand and foot, she was more than capable of hopping down from the wagon on her own.

"Thank you for getting me here safely. I trust my aunt has already paid you for my fare?" Goodness, but she hoped so! She no longer had a single penny to her name.

He nodded, and she breathed easier.

"Then this is goodnight, sir. I'll come by the livery soon to pay you a visit and meet your son." Before he could answer, she jumped down from the wagon with her travel bag clutched in her arms.

When she turned around to beam her most beauteous smile at him, he was giving her a strange look. "That's fine with me, miss, though I doubt a visit to the livery is what your aunt has in mind for your summer." He cleared his throat.

Rose's mouth fell open in surprise. "Well, I'll just have to make time for—"

"Land sakes, child!" The sharp, cultured voice interrupted their friendly farewell.

Rose glanced over at the long front veranda. A spritely looking lady was seated in a wheelchair between the double front doors which were thrown wide open. Her white hair was piled high on her head. A high-necked burgundy dress, adorned with pearlized buttons, fanned out over her knees.

She observed her niece curiously from her imperious perch. "Well, don't just stand there gawking, Rose Marie. Pick up those feet and come greet your aunt right this instant!"

With a wry glance over her shoulder, Rose shuffled her feet toward the porch. "I *will* call on you," she assured Jensen in a hushed voice before stepping out of earshot.

"Mercy me, Rose Marie Addington!" Her aunt's voice

rose to an incredulous squawk. "If you don't hurry, I might not live long enough to make your acquaintance."

Rose's glowing visions of stepping inside a storybook future shriveled to the size of an acorn. So much for her many rosy daydreams about meeting her kin for the first time. Winifred Monroe didn't sound one bit like an aging princess in a fairytale.

More like a fire-breathing dragon!

For the first time since the joy of discovering she had an aunt, Rose wondered if her mother had been justified in leaving her family and wealth behind. She drew a bracing breath, knowing she was about to find out.

Chapter 2: Intruder!

Rose

Rose moved hesitantly up the porch stairs, pausing about halfway up to turn and give Jensen another wave.

He was already circling back down the driveway and didn't look back.

"Welcome to the Bent Horseshoe Ranch, Miss Rose." A middle-aged man in a dark suit stepped away from the handles of her aunt's wheelchair to reach for Rose's travel bag. His hair was slicked back with way too much pomade, giving him an almost funereal appearance. He inclined his head respectfully at her. "Allow me to deliver your bag to your room."

She was surprised to discover that her aunt's home had a name. No doubt there was a story behind it, but now didn't feel like the time to ask.

Unaccustomed to receiving such service, she stared at the man's hand, hesitant to relinquish her bag to him. It contained her most valued possession, her manuscript. Somehow, she doubted her aunt would approve of her secret hobby.

"That's quite alright, sir." She leaned away from him, highly doubting it was feasible to juggle her bag while pushing a wheelchair, anyway. "There's no need to trouble yourself on my account."

"Oh, for pity's sake, Rose Marie!" Aunt Winifred gave her an admonishing look. "Let Rupert do his job, dear." Her voice softened as she beckoned her niece forward. "Come inside and let me get a better look at you."

Rupert proved to be up to the task of carrying Rose's travel bag while wheeling her aunt into the house, after all. Rose followed them, keeping a close watch on her bag, and found herself in an entry foyer ablaze with light.

Though it wasn't yet fully dark outside, the shadows around the cedars had been deepening around Jensen's wagon. Inside her aunt's home, however, candles galore were flickering from chandeliers overhead and a scattering of lamps, each one more ornate looking than the last. Several of them boasted globes of stained glass that sent prisms of color across the walls and ceiling.

"It's so lovely here," she sighed, then immediately wanted to bite her tongue. Her aunt did not impress her as a woman who welcomed chitchat.

"I'm glad you think so," Aunt Winifred's starchy voice wafted over her as they entered the adjoining parlor, "since you'll be living here."

Rose paused in the doorway to gaze in awe at her elegant surroundings. The pair of chandeliers in the parlor were a feat of iron architecture and wide enough to hold at least a hundred candles. She'd never before witnessed such lavishness firsthand. Had her aunt truly turned on so much light to get a better look at her impoverished niece?

She drank in the glorious floor-to-ceiling bookshelves on the far end of the room. Oh, to own so many books! It was a luxury far beyond her wildest dreams. She squinted a little, trying to read the titles on their spines. Sadly, she was standing too far away.

"At last I can see you!" Her aunt tweaked her burgundy-hued skirts out of the way to roll a few inches closer to her. "These eyes aren't what they used to be, child." She nodded a silent message to Rupert, who disappeared into the foyer with Rose's travel bag in hand.

Moments later, she heard his footfalls heading down the long hallway past the foyer, not upstairs as she'd originally assumed. "I'm no longer a child," she murmured, unable to remember if she'd shared her age in any of her letters. "I know I might not look it, ma'am, because I'm so short, but I am twenty-years-old."

"Bah!" Her aunt waved a hand dismissively. "I'm well aware of your age, dearest. Your mother wrote me the day you were born." Her discerning gaze swept Rose's threadbare gown from its neckline to its hemline.

"She did?" Rose was still grappling with the conundrum of being so abruptly whisked back into the same family dynasty that had rejected her mother all those years ago. "Then why haven't we ever met before?"

Her aunt smoothed a hand over the side of her hair, not that a single strand looked out of place. Her fingers were weighed down with rings. They had a slight tremor in them as she lowered them back to her lap. "Naturally, you are full of questions. I expected no less. Come sit with me." She waved vaguely toward a collection of blue velvet sofas and chairs. "We'll enjoy a cup of tea, and I'll answer as many of them as we have time for this evening."

Rose's stomach rumbled at the mention of tea. Utterly mortified, she clapped a hand over her midsection.

Her aunt grew still at the sound, her papery features

waxing a shade or two paler. "When was the last time you ate, Rose Marie?" Something akin to regret flashed through her gaze.

"It was back on the train, ma'am." Rose gave her a purposely vague answer. Though her insides were clawing with hunger, her pride wouldn't allow her to admit that it had been over a week since she'd enjoyed a full meal.

"What day of the week, precisely?" Her aunt snapped out the words. "The truth, dearest. I insist."

"It was yesterday," she confessed in a small voice. "Morning," she added at nearly a whisper as she backed up a few steps and took a seat on the edge of the nearest sofa. She tried and utterly failed to hold in a sigh at the shiny black pianoforte anchoring the side of the room directly across from where she was sitting. One could only hope her aunt would allow her to plink around some on its keys. She'd never before had the luxury of lessons, but she'd always wanted to learn how to play like her mother. If the poor woman hadn't caught a fever a few winters earlier, she might've finally gotten the break in her musical career she'd always hoped for.

"Mercy!" Her aunt sprang into motion, wheeling her chair straight for the chain against the far wall. She gave it several frenzied yanks. "Rupert," she called. "Rupert?" Her voice rose in agitation.

"Yes, ma'am?" Her butler's approach was so swift and silent that Rose didn't hear him coming. He simply appeared like magic in the doorway of the parlor.

"My niece is famished. Bring her a tray of everything we had for dinner. The ham, the pheasant, the potatoes, all of it!"

"Good gracious! Turning out a feast won't be necessary." Rose held up both hands. "I appreciate your kindness, but tea is more than enough this late in the day. And perhaps a few crackers?" She added the last part in a hopeful voice.

"Nonsense," her aunt retorted. "You need proper nourishment. Rupert?" She shot him a harried look that seemed to demand why he was still standing there.

"Coming right up, ma'am." He bowed and left the room as silently as he'd arrived.

"Now." Aunt Winifred rounded on Rose once again, surveying her with a troubled look. "I wish to know exactly how many meals you consumed on your train ride here."

"Please, ma'am." Rose shook her head, inwardly beseeching her to let it go. "We have much more important things to discuss. I'm bursting with so many questions that I hardly know where to begin." She waved her hands to take in the sumptuous parlor. "I suppose we could start with your collection of books. How in the world did you acquire such a marvelous library?"

"We'll get to that in time." Her aunt wheeled her chair forward to park herself directly in front of Rose. "How many meals, Rose Marie? I need to know. I *must* know!"

The journey had taken the better part of two weeks, and she'd run out of money on the fifth day. She'd tried to ration out her last meal in bite-sized portions for the remainder of the trip, but even that plan had fallen short. "I honestly do not recall, ma'am, but I had more than enough, I assure you." Sadly, her stomach chose that exact moment to growl again, underscoring the fib.

Her aunt's hands flew to her mouth. "Oh, my!" She choked out the words.

What happened next twisted Rose's heart. She was forced to watch as Aunt Winifred burst into tears. She rocked back and forth in her wheelchair, moaning some-thing incomprehensible into her fingers.

"Aunt Winifred," Rose gasped. She flew off the sofa cushion and dropped to her knees before the agonized woman. "Here, ma'am. Take this." She unearthed Jensen's handkerchief that she'd tucked inside the wrist of her sleeve earlier. She'd plumb forgotten to return it before he drove away.

"I've blubbered into it once today," she admitted wryly, "but it's otherwise clean." Or so she hoped. Was it rude to offer a person a hanky that already held a few dried tears? "Jensen lent it to me while we were on the road."

"Isn't he a dear?" Her aunt whisked the crumpled cloth from Rose's hand and dabbed the edges of her eyes with it, making a few wheezing sounds as she struggled to regain her composure. "I tried to find you," she confided in a muffled voice into the square of linen. "Unfortunately, by the time word reached me about your father's passing, you were long gone from your last known address."

It was true. Rose had sold her few belongings and procured a job at a poorhouse on the outskirts of Atlanta. Her primary task was to feed and water the chickens there, as well as gather the eggs each morning and afternoon. The rest of the time, she'd worked the fields with her fellow resi-dents, raising and harvesting beans, corn, cotton, and grain.

"I found a job near the city limits," Rose explained in a gentle voice. "I counted myself fortunate to do so." Not everyone who'd lost their homes after the war had been able to find a way to support themselves. All too many of her former friends and acquaintances had ended up on the street.

"Fortunate?" Her aunt raised her head from the hanky,

looking aghast. "You were living in a poorhouse," she reminded tartly.

"It was better than wandering the streets of Atlanta." Sad, but true. She might not have otherwise survived the past eleven months.

"Other than the fact I might have found you sooner." Her aunt's voice grew morose. "I tried to find you, dearest. I truly did. I hired the best detectives money could buy."

Rose reached for her aunt's hands. "I am most grateful that you did, ma'am." Her first impression of the woman had been sorely inaccurate. Beneath Winifred Monroe's starchy demeanor was a very tender heart.

Her aunt made another bleating sound and clapped the hanky to her eyes once again.

"If you'll point me toward the kitchen, I'd be glad to fetch you something to drink, ma'am," Rose offered anxiously. She had no idea where the kitchen was, but she'd wander the halls until she found it, if she had to.

"No, love." Aunt Winifred's voice quavered. "Rupert will be back shortly with all the refreshments we require." She lowered the hanky from her red-rimmed eyes. "Do return to the sofa. Your legs will cramp if you remain on the floor for long."

"My legs are strong, ma'am," Rose assured, in no hurry to leave her distressed relative.

She received a watery smile in return. "Well, that makes one of us." The older woman sighed as she gestured toward her own legs. "Mine have never worked right." She gave the offending appendages a quick pat of disgust. "I was born this way."

Sympathy rolled in waves through Rose as she returned to the sofa at last. She leaned forward conversationally. "Something tells me you've never let it hold you back, ma'am." She could only imagine the pity her aunt had endured over the years. The scoffing. The underestimation of her abilities, given how sharp her mind was.

"You're right." Her aunt grunted. "If only to prove to the rest of the world they were wrong about me." A glint of mischief returned to her gaze. "I cannot tell you how satisfying it's been, giving orders to grown men at the rail yard from this infernal contraption." She slapped her hands against the arms of her wheelchair for emphasis. "If nothing else, my employees have learned that leadership comes in all shapes and sizes."

"I reckon that means we're both survivors." Rose liked her aunt's gumption. "In our own ways." She suspected she'd find even more to admire in the woman as they got to know each other better. Already a sense of kinship was springing between them.

The two women stared at each other for several heartbeats, taking each other's measure. Then they broke into smiles.

"You've got my younger sister's spirit, alright." Her aunt shook a boney finger at her. "Emma was never one to back down while we were growing up. She always spoke her mind and never failed to follow her heart. Regrettably, her independent spirit wasn't something our parents understood." She shook her head sadly. "All they cared about were production numbers and dollar signs. Such things made no sense to Emma. Her heart was buried too deep in her music."

"You miss her." That undeniable fact warmed Rose's heart more than anything else her aunt had confided in her up to this point.

"I do." Aunt Winifred nodded. "I never stopped missing her. For years, I begged Father to change his mind about

Emma, but he wouldn't relent." She drew a deep breath and let it ease out of her. "He had too much Old World blood left in him, I'm afraid. It's not something the younger generations would understand, but there was a time when family names and titles mattered a lot more than they do now." She curled her fingers over the arms of her wheelchair. "Father had the perfect groom from the perfect family picked out for poor Em. Or so he thought. She could barely stand the fellow. Since I couldn't wed in my crippled state, the burden fell on her to forge a powerful alliance between two renowned shipping families." She abruptly fell silent, staring blindly across the room at nothing in particular.

It went without saying that Rose's mother had refused to hold up her end of the agreement.

"When did my mother meet my father?" she inquired softly, hoping to move their conversation back into happier territory.

"Only a few weeks before leaving town with him." Her aunt's gaze whipped back to hers, as sharp and probing as ever. "Jonas hitchhiked into town from heaven only knew where. The next thing I knew, he was courting my sister. In secret, of course. Our parents would've never approved."

"They were sweethearts." Everything her parents had subsequently sacrificed and suffered had been done in the name of love.

"They were indeed. At first, I feared Em was reading more into your father's attention than she should, out of sheer desperation to rid herself of her unwanted suitor. After a few days, though, their affections grew to the point that I actually envied what they had."

Rose blinked in surprise. She'd not expected such raw honesty from her aunt. Such a complete lack of condemnation toward her parents.

Rupert returned to the parlor, balancing a silver tray on his fingertips. Aunt Winifred's expression smoothed to one of delight. "Thank you, Rupert!" She spread her hands grandly. "Dinner is served."

Rose's emotions soared to ecstatic levels as Rupert set his tray on the coffee table with a flourish and removed the lid. A veritable feast appeared — small squares of meats, cheeses, and bread that looked and smelled freshly baked. *Glory of glories!* She drank in the generous portions of chicken, beef, pheasant, and ham arranged artfully around the tray.

He removed a smaller lid beneath the larger lid to reveal diced and steamed vegetables. There were potatoes, ornamental carrots, pole beans, and zucchini.

Rose accepted the plate and fork he handed her, feeling positively shaky from hunger. The moment her aunt finished saying grace over the food, she plunged her fork into the delectable entrees Rupert had heaped on the plate. She was too famished for any further conversation. No doubt, her manners came across as a bit rusty as she scarfed down the food, but that was something she would worry about correcting after her belly was filled.

Rupert left the room again and returned a minute or two later with a pot of steaming tea and two teacups. They were painted in a blue chintz print with rims gilded in gold that Rose suspected was real.

She ate and drank until she couldn't stuff in a single bite more. "Oh, dear!" She laid her fork on her plate and set them on the coffee table. "I might have overdone it."

"I sorely doubt it." Her aunt shook her head. "The way I see it, you have an entire week of eating to catch up on, and that's assuming you were fed properly down in Atlanta."

"I was," Rose assured. This time, she was telling the

truth. "Our accommodations were humble, but we had plenty of food on the farm. It wasn't an easy life, but it was a good one." The men and women in charge had strictly enforced their rations during the winter months, but no one had gone hungry.

Her aunt snorted. "A good life, eh? That is likely an overstatement, but I'll let it pass now that I have you back where you belong." She gave a long, gusty sigh. "It's such a pleasure to make your acquaintance at long last. I've dreamed of this day for so long." Her eyes misted with emotion all over again.

"It's an honor to meet you, too, ma'am." It felt good for Rose to belong to someone again.

Her aunt sniffed. "Feel free to drop the *ma'ams*. Aunt Winifred is good enough for me. Or Aunt Win, if you prefer to call me by what my ornery nephews have taken to calling me lately."

"Aunt Win." Rose said it aloud, very much liking the sound of the shortened version of her aunt's name. Then she spoiled the effect by yawning.

"You're exhausted." Her aunt shifted restlessly as she reached for the wheels of her chair. "Follow me. Rupert will clear our plates, while I show you to your room."

Rose glanced guiltily at the mess they were leaving behind. She wasn't accustomed to having others clean up after her. However, her aunt was an adamant creature. When she gave an order, a person was inclined to follow it.

Two women about Rose's age were waiting for them in the foyer. At the sight of her aunt, they dipped into curtsies. "Good evening, ma'am," they intoned in unison. Both were brown-eyed and possessed strawberry-blonde hair. One was an inch shorter than the other and her face was a smidgen rounder. Their uniforms were simple gray dresses, pristine white aprons, and matching white caps.

Her aunt nodded at them. "These two young women will assist you in getting unpacked and settled in. This is Clarice." She nodded at the taller woman with the oval features. "The other one is Davina. They're sisters."

Rose gaped at her aunt. "You're lending me *two* of your maids?"

"Is that a problem, niece?" Her aunt fixed a stern eye on her.

"All to myself?" Rose squeaked.

"Yes, dearest. Two. I believe I enunciated my words carefully."

Disbelieving laughter pealed out of Rose. "By any chance, does this marvel include, er..." She glanced around the room until her gaze lit on a clock resting on a marble-topped credenza. "A bath at eight o'clock in the evening?" She waved her hand beneath her nose. "You really don't wish to know how long it's been since my last soak, Aunt Win."

One of her maids made a tittering sound that ceased the moment her aunt shot them a warning look.

"This marvel, as you so colorfully stated, includes whatever you have need of, my dear. I pay my staff handsomely to upkeep my home and tend to the needs of our family."

Rose clasped her hands beneath her chin, hardly able to fathom such luxury. "Er..." She glanced at the two women, then returned her attention to her aunt, unsure how to proceed. "How does one go about delivering a request to one's maids?"

Another titter of mirth rolled through the foyer. This time, Rose was fairly certain it came from Davina. She was the shorter one, with a sprinkling of freckles across her nose that looked like someone had taken a cinnamon shaker to her.

Aunt Winifred glared another warning at the two sisters. "You don't make requests, niece. You give orders. Like this." She eyed the two young women over her spectacles. "Davina, you'll escort my niece to her room. Clarice, you'll draw her a warm bath."

"Yes, ma'am," they chorused, treating her to another curtsy.

"Oh, and Clarice?" Her aunt spread her hands. "Has Rupert finished delivering my niece's luggage to her room?"

Clarice nodded. "Yes, ma'am."

"All of it?"

Clarice looked puzzled. "There was only one bag, ma'am."

"Only one bag?" Aunt Win cast a questioning look at Rose. "Did ol' Jensen up and drive away without delivering the rest of your belongings to us?"

Rose shook her head nervously. "The farm where I've been staying had very strict rules about economizing. The dress I have on is the only one I own."

Her aunt swallowed hard. "I see." Her expression clearly stated that she didn't. "Well, then, I suppose I'll add the dressmaker's shop to our list of places to visit tomorrow."

"Our list?" Rose's eyes widened.

Her aunt smiled. "Yes. You'll be seeing a dance master, a singing instructor, and the headmistress of a finishing school. She lives a few streets over, but she's agreed to stop by here once a week to administer lessons in deportment. Your painting lessons will begin the following Monday. A week after that, I've arranged for a Latin tutor to meet with you."

As much as Rose appreciated all her aunt was doing for

her, her heart sank as she heard the plans unfold — plans that were clearly designed to give her a much-needed layer of social polish. As much as she needed all the coaching and mentoring, when on earth was she going to find time to finish copying her manuscript?

It was a puzzle she'd have to figure out.

"Thank you, Aunt Win," she murmured softly. "Everything you've arranged for me sounds lovely." She motioned for Davina to lead the way from the parlor. "Goodnight, ma'am."

"Goodnight, dearest." Her aunt watched her shrewdly as she marched into the hallway on the heels of her maids.

The hallway was dimly lit by wall sconces flickering with yet more candles. "Your aunt's suite is at the end of the hall," Davina explained. "Yours is next to hers. Here." She threw open the door to a bedroom so lavishly furnished that Rose gasped.

"*This* is where I'll be staying?" She stepped inside, pinching the top of one arm, half expecting to wake up and find herself back at the poorhouse in Atlanta.

Clarice disappeared around a silk screen, and the sound of splashing water ensued.

"Yes, ma'am." Davina gave a bounce of delight in her black lace-up boots. "It's one of the loveliest suites in the house. It comes with a real feather mattress, a dressing room, a powder room with a tub, and a private lounge for reading and relaxing." She lowered her voice to a conspiratorial note. "Once, when a senator visited our town, his twin daughters stayed overnight in these very rooms!"

Rooms. Not a single bedroom, but rooms as in plural.

It was almost too much to take in. Rose reached for the edge of the nearest piece of furniture, which happened to be an antique white dresser.

"Are you well, ma'am?" Davina eyed her with concern. When Rose didn't answer, she inquired in a more urgent voice, "Miss Addington? Should I fetch your aunt? Or a doctor?"

It took a nearly superhuman effort for Rose to collect her scattered emotions, but she was made of sterner stuff. "No, thank you." She straightened her spine and smoothed her hands down her wrinkled gown. "You may call me Rose, by the way."

Davina blinked several times. "Oh no, Miss Addington! We couldn't possibly take such liberties."

"According to my aunt, you don't take requests." Rose attempted to train a stern eye on her new maids and nearly broke into a chuckle. "You take orders. Therefore, I am ordering both of you to call me Rose."

"Oh, miss!" Davina shook her head, looking perplexed. "You do realize your aunt will have our heads if she over-hears us addressing you with such familiarity?"

"Then you are hereby ordered not to ever let her hear it. To preserve your necks, you may call me Rose in private."

Clarice bustled back into the room. "Your bath is drawn, Miss Addington."

"Rose," she corrected. "As Davina and I just finished discussing, the two of you are to call me Rose when we are alone."

At the maid's look of shock, Rose smiled. "Davina will explain." She unbuttoned her travel-worn gown as she saun-tered around the silk screen on the side of the bedroom. The door to the powder room stood open, and a clawfoot tub awaited her there. Steam rose from the perfume scented water.

It was sheer heaven to rinse her journey from her skin at

long last. An array of soaps and lotions rested on a tray atop a nearby chair.

"Would you like help washing your hair, Miss, er... Rose?" Clarice inquired softly from the other side of the screen.

"No, but I thank you for the offer." Rose wasn't quite ready for that level of service. Not to mention, her modesty wouldn't allow it.

"You are welcome, for sure," the woman returned warmly.

"I've laid out a towel and a nightgown on the bench behind the tub," Clarice added eagerly, "and I'm about to pull back your bed covers."

"Thank you, both of you. You've done more than enough for me this evening." Rose couldn't resist sliding her entire body beneath the water to rinse the suds from her hair. She'd never in her life enjoyed such a warm, luxurious, and unhurried bath.

Please, God, if this is a dream, don't let me wake up. I never want to wake from this.

She slowly pushed herself to a sitting position once again, just as a scream split the air.

"Davina?"

The scream was Davina's. Rose was sure of it. A whimper of alarm followed.

Rose splashed out of the tub, sloshing water everywhere in her haste to snatch up her towel. She rubbed herself partially dry, then yanked on a robe. She wrapped it around her as she ran into the bedroom. "Davina? Where are you?"

Neither Clarice nor Davina remained in the room. A quick peek into the hallway revealed Davina was standing right outside her door. She stood trembling from head to toe with her hands clenching and unclenching at her sides.

31

"Not another step, Miss Rose," she called in a low, terse voice. "There's an intruder in the foyer. Since we keep all the doors and windows locked, I'm not sure how he got inside."

Aunt Winifred's irate voice grated down the long hallway, reaching their ears. "Who are you, and what are you doing in my home?"

Rose crept closer to her maid to peer around her shoulder. Her eyes nearly bugged out at the sight of her crippled aunt brandishing a hard bound book like a weapon at a man in dusty overalls.

"Please forgive me, ma'am," the stranger stuttered, backing away from her with both hands in the air. "I'm the new delivery man at the mercantile. I tried knocking on the door, but no one answered. When I realized it was unlocked, I thought it would be better to set the food inside, so it wouldn't spoil."

"Why are you here so late?" Aunt Winifred snapped.

"Because Billy Tanner fell sick earlier today and ran behind on his deliveries. I'm taking over where he left off, trying to catch up."

"And who might you be?" She rolled nearer to him to shake her book beneath his nose.

"John Jones, ma'am. I'm one of the farmers who grows the produce you've been ordering."

Aunt Winifred slowly lowered her book. "What you are, John Jones, is a very fortunate man." She slapped the book against her leg, making him flinch. "Fortunate that you caught me with a book in hand instead of my six-shooter. As much as I enjoy consuming your produce, the next time you pay a visit to my home, you will knock. And if no one answers, you will carry your delivery away and return with it the next day. Are we clear on our new arrangement?"

"Yes, ma'am." He took another nervous step backwards toward the door.

"Good." She pointed at the door. "You may go now."

The terrified young farmer dashed from the foyer, leaving the front door gaping.

Rupert, who'd slipped quietly into the room while her aunt was threatening the intruder, hurried past her to close and lock it. "My deepest apologies, ma'am. I thought I'd locked up already."

Her aunt's expression was hard to read. "An unlocked door is still a far cry from an invitation to simply let oneself inside." She swiveled around to glance down the hallway at Rose and Davina. "And a robe, my dear niece, is not the proper attire in which to face an intruder." Her voice softened as she brandished her book in the air again. "Any more than a collection of poems is a proper weapon." She sighed and hugged the book to her chest. "It appears we have yet another stop to make tomorrow. The gunsmith's shop."

Rose's heartbeat increased. Did that mean they would be paying a visit to the handsome Lancaster Tracy? She certainly hoped so! How many gunsmith's shops could there be in a town this small?

To cover her nervousness, she inquired in a teasing voice, "I gather you don't yet own that six-shooter you mentioned, Aunt Win?"

Her aunt's mouth quirked upward at the corners. "Not yet, dearest, but I will by tomorrow."

Chapter 3: A Lovely Customer
Lancaster

When Lancaster opened his shop the next morning, he was still thinking about the woman in the blue calico dress that Jensen had driven into town the night before. She was new to Cedar Falls. That he was sure of. Life on the road as a bounty hunter had sharpened his skill at remembering things like names and faces, and her face was an unforgettable one. All night long, he'd been unable to get her porcelain features, shy smile, or fluttery wave out of his mind.

Her manner had struck him as both kindhearted and guileless. There weren't enough of those things going around these days, certainly not in his line of business. He wondered who she was as he turned the *Closed* sign on his front door to *Open*. Marching back to the counter, he opened his cash register and counted his starting cash supply for the day.

As he continued to ponder the identity of the woman in the blue dress, his thoughts inevitably drifted to Boston, where his parents and younger brother still resided. Five years ago on his twenty-first birthday, his parents had attempted to arrange a marriage between him and a woman he barely knew. As best as he could tell, the arranged marriage was an attempt to consolidate their families' rival hotel chains. When he'd refused to marry for such a mercenary reason, his father had threatened to disown him.

Lancaster had ultimately disowned his family before they could disown him, by packing a single bag and abandoning his childhood home in the dead of night. It hadn't been easy, living on the road from meal to meal and paycheck to paycheck. However, he'd thrown his lot in with a group of bounty hunters, which had helped toughen him up. They'd also taught him how to size up a man's intentions at a quick glance, improve his shooting skills, and think on his feet.

He'd developed into a man he didn't regret looking at in the mirror each morning while he shaved. A man who owned his own gunsmith shop and was beholden to nobody. Most importantly, he was no longer under the thumb of his social climbing parents who'd sworn he wouldn't amount to a thing without their suffocating assistance.

The door bell jingled, signaling he had a customer. He looked up from his cash register and grew still as the woman he'd been daydreaming about entered his shop.

She was even more enchanting up close than she'd been in the wagon. Her hair was the shade of almonds, and her eyes were as blue-green as the water gushing across the Atlantic.

Equally fascinating was the fact that she wasn't alone.

She was pushing the wheelchair of the legendary Miss Winifred Monroe, a wealthy old spinster who lived in a mansion up the road. He'd heard all sorts of interesting tidbits about her from the townsfolk. Some were flattering. Some were not.

From what he could gather, she was a tough task master over the local rail yard, though she paid her employees generously. According to some accounts, she was too outspoken and opinionated for a woman. Then again, how many females owned and operated a rail yard? He suspected it had something to do with the number of men who'd been gutted from their town's ranks during the war, but what did he know? It was the first time he'd had the pleasure of making her acquaintance.

"You must be Mr. Lancaster Tracy." Miss Monroe wasted no words, immediately living up to her reputation of being outspoken.

"The one and only, ma'am," he drawled, pushing his cash drawer shut with a metallic click. "Who's asking?" He'd long since mastered the art of direct speaking, himself.

Her eyes widened slightly at the question, clearly taken aback that he didn't already know who she was. Which he did, of course.

However, her surprise wasn't followed by the hauteur that normally accompanied a woman of wealth and privilege. She recovered her aplomb quicker than expected and briskly launched into introductions. "I'm Winifred Monroe, and this is my niece, Rose Marie." Without pausing to shake hands, exchange pleasantries, or brag about the business she owned, she got straight to the reason for their visit. "We suffered a home intrusion yesterday after my niece's arrival in town. Naturally, we're interested in purchasing two reliable pistols to protect ourselves against a repeat scenario."

All thoughts of anything but their safety fled Lancaster's mind. He bolted out from behind the cash register counter. "Were you or anyone in your household harmed in any way?" He seemed to recall someone mentioning that Miss Monroe employed an army of servants. He shot a quick glance at the door, fully prepared to hightail it down the street to the sheriff's office, if necessary.

Looking inordinately pleased, Miss Monroe gave him a bold once over, making no effort to hide the fact that she was doing so. "We suffered no injuries. Be assured I gave him the set-down of his life. He took off at a gallop afterward."

"I'm glad to hear it." Though his shoulders relaxed, he continued to scowl in concern at her. "Did you report the incident to Sheriff Snyder?" An intruder was still an intruder.

Gripping the handles of her aunt's wheelchair more tightly, Rose's perfect petal lips parted in a protest. "It wasn't necessary, sir. The man in question was simply—"

"Why, Rose Marie Addington!" Her aunt wagged an admonishing finger at her. "Do not think to defend that dusty farmer! He had no right to enter our home just because Rupert left the door unlocked."

Lancaster watched in pure male admiration as Rose's cheeks turned a delightful shade of pink. "My only point is that we were never in any danger, my dear aunt. By the time he completed his delivery, he was more afraid of us than we were of him." Despite her obvious mortification at being publicly called out on her position, she didn't hesitate to defend it.

Miss Monroe's niece was tougher than she looked, which ratcheted up Lancaster's interest in her all the more. She might be the poor relation to the Monroe dynasty, but she had spirit. He could relate to that all too well.

"The fact remains," the elderly Miss Monroe waved a hand that possessed a slight tremor, "our home was invaded, and we were fortunate the incident ended as well as it did."

She returned her attention to Lancaster with such vehemence that he was half tempted to take a step back. However, he held his ground. "What if it hadn't been a bumbling delivery man, Mr. Tracy? What if it had been a real criminal, one who intended us harm?"

He nodded gravely, though he didn't want to even consider the possibility of the lovely Rose Marie Addington and her family suffering harm of any sort. "You have every right to be concerned, ma'am."

He nodded apologetically at her niece to let her know he meant no offense at contradicting her equally valid point. It was impressive that she'd sized up the situation and determined there was no immediate danger. Clearly, she was both clever and able to perform under pressure. "You have a household staff to protect and a niece who I can tell is very precious to you."

Rose's blush deepened as she met and held his gaze for an extended moment.

It nearly caused Lancaster physical pain to break eye contact with her in order to return his attention to her aunt. The older woman's expression had grown several degrees softer. "You are entirely correct, Mr. Tracy. Please assure me you are equipped to properly arm us." She eagerly surveyed the display case of firearms housed beneath his cash register.

Everyone had a weakness. Lancaster was tickled to pieces at how quickly he'd been able to uncover Winifred Monroe's. Despite her niece's shabby appearance, she was, indeed, important to the woman. Perhaps ol' Winifred Monroe's heart wasn't as bullet proof as a few of the gossips in town had made it out to be.

He studied her shrewdly. "You've come to the right place, ma'am. I'm happy to equip you ladies to defend yourselves, should the necessity ever arise." *Which I sorely hope it does not.*

Miss Monroe made a shooting motion with both thumbs and forefingers. "As I stated before, I'd like to purchase a pair of ladies' pistols."

Sadly, *ladies' pistols* wasn't a term he was familiar with. "Ladies' pistols," he repeated carefully, assuming she meant something small. "I don't suppose you have something more specific in mind?"

At her raised eyebrows, he prodded, "Any particular type, ma'am?"

Her blank expression told him she didn't know the first thing about weaponry.

He hid his amusement by clearing his throat. "How about I jump right in to a description of my inventory, and we'll take it from there?"

Her jerky up-down nod was accompanied by a faint huff of relief.

He plunged straight into the topic. "There are a variety of Colt models on the market, presuming you'd prefer a handgun, which," he arched one eyebrow at her, "I highly recommend over the bulk and weight of a rifle."

"But of course!" She frowned in concentration, absorbing every detail as he went on to describe his collection of handguns in the display case in front of her. She looked like she was weighing and dissecting every word that came out of his mouth. When he finished, she quickly demanded, "What other weapons do you have in stock, young man?"

Rose caught his eye and gave him a grateful smile that told him she appreciated the way he was handling her aunt.

He smiled back. He couldn't help it. There was just something about her smile that made a fellow want to return it. "Well, there's the good old-fashioned Derringer." While he answered Miss Monroe's question, he remained strongly aware of Rose's gaze on him. It was a feeling that he liked. "Then there's a revolver that Remington puts out that a lot of folks seem to like. Plus, I happen to have a third little darling on hand called the Webley Bull Dog. It's a five-shot pocket revolver and the smallest piece I have in stock. I assume you're looking for a piece to carry around in your reticule?" He cocked his head at her.

"Indeed we are." The elderly woman nodded shrewdly. "I especially like the sound of that Webley Bull Dog."

He wasn't surprised. She reminded him of a bulldog herself, at least as far as her temperament went.

"But Aunt Win!" Rose looked mildly distressed as Lancaster prepared to close the deal. "That sounds danger-ous. What if one of the guns were to go off while we're carrying them? What if we end up shooting someone by mistake?"

She and her aunt exchanged a worried glance.

"You make a valid point," Lancaster assured smoothly. "That's why most of the stock I sell comes with a safety." He unlocked the display case and reached inside it to lift out a Colt. He proceeded to demonstrate how easy it was to unclick and reclick the safety button. Keeping the barrel of the Colt pointed at the floor, he showed them that it was impossible to press the trigger while the safety was engaged.

"Well, that certainly answers my niece's questions to *my* satisfaction." Miss Monroe gave a decided nod.

When Rose remained silent, Lancaster moved back behind the counter, laid down the Colt, and pulled one of the Webley Bull Dogs from the display case to his right. "Since you ladies are looking to purchase two of these, I'm happy to toss in some free shooting lessons to show my appreciation." As a general rule, he aimed to over-deliver on his customers' expectations. The very lovely one standing in front of him with an anxious wrinkle in the middle of her forehead was no exception. He angled his head casually at the wall behind him. "I have an indoor shooting range in the adjoining room."

Winifred Monroe's gaze snapped with curiosity. "How many lessons would that entail?"

He normally charged a flat fee for three thirty-minute sessions. However, he was too interested in getting to know Rose better to put a limit on the time they spent together.

"As many as it takes to get you comfortable with your new weapons." It wouldn't crush his soul if it took the woman's niece several days to master the art of shooting. Or weeks. Or months, for that matter. He couldn't wait to begin her training. There was just something about her freshly washed and pressed faded blue dress that tugged at every last one of his heartstrings.

Miss Winifred Monroe might sleep on a mattress stuffed with dollar bills, but her niece was clearly from an impoverished background. How she'd come to live under the same roof as her wealthy aunt was a matter that intrigued him enormously. He could only hope she was in town to stay.

He and her aunt engaged in another silent duel of gazes.

"Sold!" She reached up to slap her hand against the counter, looking as if she'd just made the bargain of a lifetime. "We'll need some bullets, too."

And she had. Lancaster couldn't remember the last time he'd been in such a generous mood. He rang up her purchases and tried not to choke when the woman opened her reticule and paid the full amount in cash. It bothered him to note she'd been carrying around such a large sum.

He hoped she didn't make a habit of it. Even when a person was armed, it wasn't a good idea to bandy about so much cash.

After he closed his money drawer and wrote out her receipt, her gaze twinkled knowingly at him. "How soon may we begin our lessons?"

His gaze returned to her niece. "How does tomorrow morning sound? Eight o'clock sharp?" He couldn't wait to get started.

"We'll be here." Miss Monroe reached for the timepiece dangling from the waist of her lavender silk gown. "Our visit to your shop has taken longer than expected, not that I mind." Her tone was brisk. "It was important that you took the time to explain everything in such exquisite detail to us." She reached for the box containing their twin Webley Bull Dog pistols. "Nevertheless, we are running late to our next appointment with the dressmaker." He didn't get the impression she was trying to make him feel guilty about the time they'd spent together. She was simply stating facts.

Regardless, he wasn't entirely finished taking up her time. Keeping a hand splayed over the box, he forced her to look up at him as she tugged on it in an attempt to slip it from beneath his grasp. "There's one lesson I insist on giving every new gun owner before leaving my shop, ma'am. It's the shortest and easiest one, as well as the most important one." He paused for emphasis. "Every weapon is loaded, even when it's not."

She nodded soberly. "A valuable lesson, indeed. I won't be forgetting it."

"Nor will I," Rose chimed in softly. "Thank you, sir."

Lancaster, he corrected inside his head. If they'd been alone, he would've invited her to call him by his first name. However, he doubted her oh-so-proper aunt would approve of him taking such liberties during their first encounter. As much as he longed to hear her niece speak his name in her musical alto, it would have to wait. Fortunately, her first shooting lesson would take place in the morning. He could only hope the opportunity to deepen their acquaintance would present itself at that time.

Miss Monroe once again attempted to tug the box free from his grasp.

Again, he kept a hand resting on it. "If you'd prefer, I could have the pistols delivered to your home later today, ma'am." He winked at her. "By a man who will knock and wait for you to open your door before entering the premises, I assure you."

She gave a cackle of mirth and lowered her hand from the counter. "Bring them yourself, and I'll have my cook brew up a pot of her prized coffee from the Orient.

"Now *that's* tempting!" Coffee was his weakness, second only to a certain pair of blue-green eyes in the room that were studying him in feminine confusion.

"It was supposed to be," Winifred Monroe returned in a matter-of-fact voice. "A good day to you, Mr. Tracy. We look forward to seeing you and the Bull Dogs at, say, half past five? I reckon that'll get you beyond your closing time?"

"It will." He nodded. "I'll be there as long as I don't get a flood of last-minute customers that keep me late." If it had been anyone but the crotchety Miss Monroe extending the invitation, he might've wondered if she had her eye on him as a potential beau for her niece. According to the locals, there'd been a scarcity of eligible bachelors in town since the war. However, the wealthy rail yard owner sitting in front of him probably considered any relation of hers to be well out of his league. She was likely only being kind and welcoming to him as a newcomer in town. It was equally possible she considered a man who owned as many weapons as he did a wise ally to make.

"The coffee will keep, even if you're running a little late." Though her tone was dismissive, her offer was unexpectedly magnanimous.

"Thank you, ma'am." He inclined his head respectfully before hurrying around the counter. Moving ahead of Rose, he held open the door for the two women.

Rose offered him another one of her shy smiles as she rolled her aunt past him.

A light summer breeze swirled through the door, sending a whiff of her flowery scent his way. He stared after her, wondering if their forthcoming visit to the dressmaker's shop was for her or her aunt. He reckoned he'd find out soon.

Closing the door, he unabashedly continued watching them through the picture window as they slowly crossed Main Street and continued moving up the sidewalk. A few doors down, he saw them pause in front of the Beaumont sisters' clothing boutique.

Don't get too fancied up now. Something twisted in Lancaster's gut at the thought of Rose Marie Addington wearing anything other than her plain blue calico the next time he saw her. A woman's attire was a powerful thing, not completely unlike a weapon. A new dress had the ability to render a complete metamorphosis in her appearance.

And he happened to like the lovely Miss Addington exactly the way she was. He could only hope that her strong-willed aunt didn't intend to turn her into something else entirely.

Chapter 4: Fitting In
Rose

I t was late in the afternoon, and Rose was mentally exhausted by the time she and her aunt returned home. Servants marched to and from their carriage, transporting mountains of packages in their arms. Never in her life had she been on a shopping excursion like the one they'd just completed. It made her uncomfortable that her aunt had spent so much money. It made her even more uncomfortable that the dear creature had spent every penny of it on her long-lost niece.

"It's too much," she protested for the dozenth time. "You outdid yourself and then some, ma'am." She could never hope to repay such exorbitant generosity, not if she worked her fingers to the bone for the rest of her days.

"Nonsense! You had need of a few items, and we took care of it. That is all." Her aunt ignored her gasp of disbelief as they waited for Rupert to hand over the team of horses to one of the ranch hands. He swiftly took his place behind her wheelchair and rolled her toward the long side ramp leading up to the front veranda.

Rose took the shorter route up the stairs, fearing her hair

was going to slide out of its pins at any moment. She'd lost count of the number of times she'd bumped and loosened them earlier while trying on hat after hat and garment after garment.

She was now the cautiously grateful owner of five new gowns. *Five!* It was an unheard of luxury that she'd protested every step of the way. Her aunt had ignored her and continued to shop as if driven by demons.

Only one of the gowns had been close enough to Rose's exact measurements to alter and send home with them today. The fact that her aunt had paid extra to do so had utterly robbed Rose of her breath. It was as if the woman had money to burn!

Despite her many misgivings over being the recipient of such extravagance, Rose couldn't wait to don the new gown. It was a lightweight white cotton sprinkled with delicate lavender petals. It boasted a round neckline with a lace inset, an attractively ruched bodice, and a skirt that was full enough to require a petticoat. It was, by far, her favorite of all their purchases today. The other four gowns would be delivered over the next several days — an emerald green riding habit, a sky blue ball gown, a pink morning dress, and a frivolously layered gown the color of daffodils that would be suitable for any number of occasions from church services to tea parties.

They'd also purchased a variety of hats, gloves, scarves, shawls, reticules, boots, and dress shoes in addition to a robe, a pair of nightgowns, stockings, and a whole pile of unmentionables. Rose's head was spinning with the enormity of just how much and how quickly her life was changing. It was approaching dinnertime, and her head was positively aching from her first day of pampering.

"Are you ill?" Her aunt gave her an anxious look as they entered the foyer.

"Not at all, Aunt Win. I'm simply..." Rose gazed around the lavishly decorated walls, trying to find the right words to express what she was feeling, "a little overwhelmed, I suppose." She crinkled her eyes at her aunt. "So much is happening so quickly." She did not wish to appear ungrateful. However, it was impossible to pretend like she was at peace with everything that was happening.

"I imagine it does feel a bit overwhelming." Her aunt studied her critically. Then she snapped her fingers. "Davina? Clarice?" She glanced around them impatiently until the two sisters appeared and took their places in front of her. "I trust you know how to make my niece comfortable before dinner?" She took out her watch piece again. "We have a guest arriving in less than an hour. I wish for my niece to look and feel her best."

"Yes, ma'am," they chorused, bobbing curtsies and inclining their strawberry-blonde heads at her. Their white ruffled aprons were so pressed, starched, and spotless that Rose could only presume they'd recently donned fresh ones.

The two sisters bustled Rose down the hallway to her room. The moment the door was shut, she rounded on them. "I know you're here at the behest of my aunt, but all I truly desire is a moment alone." She glanced longingly toward her bed.

"Oh, no, Miss Addington!" Clarice regretfully followed her gaze. "There's no time for a nap."

"Rose," Rose shot back in a more agitated voice than she intended. "You agreed to call me Rose when we are alone." She desperately needed someone in her new household to treat her like a normal person.

"Yes, of course! My apologies, ma'am." Clarice looked so distressed that Rose nearly burst into tears.

"Please forgive me," she bleated, wondering if her aunt had already managed to spoil her good manners during her first twenty-four hours in residence. "I had no right to snap at you. It's just that my head is pounding something awful, and the whole world is spinning." Her voice trembled with emotion as she silently begged the young woman to understand. *We're nearly the same age. We're not so different, you and I.* Only a few short days ago, she'd ranked lower in this world than the two sisters who'd been assigned to wait hand and foot on her.

"It's perfectly understandable." Davina made a clucking sound and inserted her shorter frame between the two of them. She gently gripped Rose's elbow and used it to tow her to a chaise lounge on the far side of the room. "You're unaccustomed to being bandied about like an animal on display at a fair."

A moan escaped Rose as she waved at the mountain of hat boxes and other packages piled in the center of the room, waiting to be unpacked. "I know it's despicable of me to complain, but I cannot imagine any poor animal being forced to try on so many fripperies in a single afternoon." It felt downright inhumane. "I don't know how I'm ever going to wear all of them. I'm not accustomed to such things." She felt exhausted to her very soul at the thought of being trussed up like a Christmas turkey in so many layers.

"You're right. Not even an animal would want to be decked out so in this summer heat." Davina's gaze followed Rose's agitated wave at the pile of packages. Then she did the unthinkable. She neighed like a horse, a sound she quickly followed with the moo of a cow.

Clarice grinned and added the snort of a piglet to the mix. She dissolved into laughter before she finished.

Rose, who'd been discreetly dabbing at the corners of her eyes, spluttered out a chuckle.

Davina attempted to keep a straight face, but she eventually broke down and joined in the explosion of merriment.

For the next few minutes, all three of them took turns baa-ing, clucking, honking, twittering, barking, meowing, and baying every animal sound they could think of. They were soon laughing so hard they were unable to continue. Their eyes were positively streaming from it.

Clarice was the first one to regain any modicum of composure. "Miss Monroe is going to skin us alive and boil us for dinner if we don't straighten up our act, and soon."

For some reason, her comment sent them into another round of hilarity.

Davina stumbled to the washbasin, half bent over laughing, and returned with a cool, damp cloth in hand. "Here you go, my friend."

Friend? Rose stared at her, open-mouthed.

Davina flushed and sobered. "I, er, didn't mean—"

"You better have meant it." Rose clung to the word like a lifeline. "I could sorely use a friend right now."

"Good, because you have two new friends in my sister and me, if that's what you truly want." Though Davina's voice was teasing, her expression remained cautious. "In private, of course," she added hastily. "I highly doubt your aunt would approve."

"Oh, but I do want that," Rose sighed. "No one else in the world has ever made me laugh with such abandon. That was better than medicine." Her head was aching less severely, and she was starting to relax.

"You're welcome. Now help save our hides by allowing us to get you all fancied up for dinner." Motioning for Rose to lie back on the chaise lounge, Davina draped the cool cloth over her swollen eyelids. Then she started snapping out orders to her sister.

"Hang her new gown on the wire dress form. Then fetch us a pair of kettles from the kitchen. We'll have those folds steamed out in no time."

"Thank you," Rose whispered, clutching the cold compress tighter over her eyes. "Both of you."

Davina playfully swatted her hands away. "You're supposed to be helping save our hides. At the moment, that entails sitting there like a pampered princess no matter how much it cramps your southern sensibilities."

From the other side of the room, Clarice bleated like a billy goat before heading out the door.

Rose started laughing again, silently this time. "I'm so glad my aunt found me and brought me to Cedar Falls," she sighed. "Otherwise, I would've never met the two of you."

"Or the handsome gunsmith who'll be serving as your guest this evening," Davina pointed out in a sly voice.

Rose felt her face turn red. "How in the world did you—?"

"Ha!" Davina swapped out the fast-warming cloth for a cooler, damper one. "Rupert may look dignified, but he gossips worse than an old fish wife when he's out of your aunt's earshot."

"I would've never guessed," Rose mused in a wondering voice. "He comes across as so prim and proper."

"That's for your aunt's benefit," Davina assured with a knowing snort. "He's much less dignified when she's not around. Why, if he'd been in the room a few minutes ago, mark my words, he'd have been growling like a bear and howling like a wolf."

"He's very kind and doting on my aunt." Rose believed in giving credit where credit was due. "Though she tries to hide it, I suspect she's quite fond of him."

"Oh, she is," Davina agreed, "and he's equally fond of her. They've been at each other's sides since she was in the cradle. They're very loyal to each other."

Unless Rose was mistaken, she detected a bit of affection in Davina's voice for the outspoken, opinionated older woman. Before she could comment on it, Clarice breezed back into the room and shut the door.

"Mr. Tracy is the talk of the town," she sighed wistfully. "You are most fortunate to have caught his attention, Rose."

"I don't believe I did any such thing," Rose protested, blushing again. "My aunt merely purchased a pair of pistols from his shop earlier today. That is all."

"That is all." Clarice repeated her words mockingly. "Other than the fact that he's personally delivering said pistols and joining you for dinner. When all the wishful young ladies and their wishful mamas hear about this, you're going to be the talk of Cedar Falls. Mark my words."

"Perish the thought!" Rose abruptly straightened, allowing the damp cloth to slip from her eyes.

Davina caught it with a chuckle. "Get used to the attention, my dear. You'd have been the talk of the town, anyway, for no other reason than you're Miss Monroe's long-lost niece."

Rose pressed her hands to her bosom, trying to tamp down on a fresh round of nerves. "I'm the daughter of a humble railway worker and a harpsichordist." One who never made her debut on stage. "I refuse to pretend to be anything more than I am."

Davina made a scoffing sound. "Whether you like it or not, my new friend, you're also kin to the richest woman in town. It will open more doors for you than you can imagine. You might as well settle in and enjoy the attention."

"Along with Mr. Tracy's company," Clarice added with a breathless titter. "I've never met him. Is he as handsome as they say he is?"

Rose mulled over the question for a moment. "His features are...arresting." She felt her face growing warm at the memory of visiting with him earlier. He possessed the kind of features a girl had a hard time getting out of her mind. Strong and chiseled.

"Yes, sister dear." Davina sounded amused. "The answer is yes. Our lovely Rose finds Mr. Lancaster Tracy exceedingly handsome."

Rose made a face at her. "Now you're putting words in my mouth."

"Am I?" Davina gave her a coy look.

Fortunately, Clarice chose that moment to announce that Rose's new gown was ready to don. She spent the next several minutes being tucked, prodded, buttoned, combed, and otherwise transformed into a lady of society.

She stared dazedly at herself in the mirror when Clarice and Davina were finished. "I hardly recognize myself." She wasn't sure if that was a good thing.

"You'll get used to it," Davina declared softly. "In time."

Rose wasn't so sure. Her weariness from earlier returned as Davina silently led her down the hallway to the dining room. She paused beneath the arched doorway, staring at a long elegant table that could easily seat a dozen or more people.

"There you are!" Aunt Winifred was already presiding

at the head of the table. She gestured for Rose to claim the chair on her right.

Rupert appeared and pulled the chair out for her. Davina gave her a gentle nudge from behind to get her moving toward it.

Swallowing nervously, Rose stepped further into the room to face her aunt. "Thank you." Her voice came out strangely high-pitched. "For the new gown. For everything."

Her aunt made a harrumphing sound. "You don't look too happy about it."

"Oh, but I am," Rose assured hastily. "I'm merely tired. It was a long journey west from Atlanta." As she took the seat Rupert was so kindly holding out for her, her thoughts drifted to the lame and elderly friends she'd left behind at the poorhouse. How they would've enjoyed eating in a room as fine and as elegant as this! She glanced up at the crystal chandeliers flickering with candles overhead. It was a room fit for royalty.

"Are you listening to a word I'm saying?" her aunt demanded out of the blue.

Rose ducked her head guiltily at the realization that her aunt had been speaking since the moment she'd taken a seat beside her. "I reckon not, ma'am. My mind was wandering."

To her surprise, the older woman chuckled. "Well, I did ask for your honesty."

A clatter in the hallway outside the dining room made Rose tense. Had Lancaster Tracy finally arrived?

"Fashionably late, as usual, my dearest Anna Kate." There was a world of affection in Aunt Winifred's voice.

Anna Kate? Rose's gaze flew to the newcomer in the room. She found herself staring at a true southern belle. The stunning young woman possessed long, doll-like curls and was tucked into a ruffled pink gown that reminded Rose of cake and icing.

"Do not stand on my account," she pleaded when Rose started to scoot back her chair. "I'm your cousin, Anna Kate Armstrong, and I couldn't be more delighted to meet you." She glided toward Rose with a hand outstretched.

Ignoring her cousin's insistence that she remain seated, Rose shot to her feet. "Pleased to meet you. I'm Rose Marie Addington." She lightly clasped Anna Kate's hand, swimming with uncertainty on the inside. She couldn't help wondering what her cousin thought about having a long-lost family member pop out of the woodwork. Did she resent all the attention their aunt had been giving her?

However, she could see nothing but curiosity burning in Anna Kate's gaze as she tugged her closer for a hug. "If you insist on standing, you might as well give me a proper greeting," she murmured against her shoulder. "You don't know how painful it is to be the only sister with three ornery brothers. It's so good to have another female in the family."

Rose was smiling by the time Anna Kate stepped back. "I'm happy to help even up the numbers." Her cousin's hug had gone a long way toward setting her at ease.

"I'm sorry my husband couldn't make it this evening." Anna Kate claimed the chair across from Rose. They both took their seats. "He was detained on business. However, he is every bit as anxious to make your acquaintance as my brothers are."

Your husband? Rose reckoned that explained why Anna Kate's last name was Armstrong instead of Monroe.

"Everyone will be here for lunch after church on Sunday," Aunt Winifred announced. "Rose can meet the rest of our family then."

"I can't wait," Rose murmured faintly. *Our family.* In

the past few days, she'd gone from believing she was alone in the world to having four cousins and an uncle. And now she had her cousin's husband as extended family.

A light knock sounded on the doorframe. "Our guest has arrived," Rupert announced in his most formal voice.

Rose wiggled uncomfortably, hardly daring to raise her gaze.

"Lancaster!" Anna Kate's voice rang with familiarity, greeting the local gunsmith like an old friend. "I see someone managed to pry you out of your dark, boorish cave at long last. I can't wait to tell Gregory." She chuckled merrily. "Then again, he might not believe it unless he sees it for himself." Her laughing gaze landed on her new cousin. "You'd best join us for lunch on Sunday. Otherwise, my husband might accuse me of carrying tales."

"If that's a genuine invitation, ladies," Lancaster Tracy drawled as he moved toward Aunt Winifred and clasped her hand.

"Indeed, it is," she assured. "My rascally youngest nephews, Will and Grady, were fit to be tied when they found out you were joining us for dinner. However, their pa has them too busy working in the rail yard this evening to break away for dinner." She spread her heavily be-ringed hands, gesturing for Mr. Tracy to take a seat beside Rose. "Expanding a railroad spur is hard work. I'm mighty grateful for their assistance."

"I heard about that, ma'am." The gunsmith nodded admiringly at her. "I, for one, will greatly appreciate the decreased shipping times for supplies coming from the west coast."

"You're welcome, Mr. Tracy." Aunt Winifred sounded supremely satisfied over the prospect of providing such a needed service to her town.

"Lancaster." He inclined his head respectfully at her. "Please. I'm not accustomed to standing on ceremony with my friends." He cast an admiring sideways glance at Rose.

Though she felt his gaze on her, it took an extra second or two for her to work up the courage to meet his gaze. The same current of awareness that had been between them earlier was still there. It was all she could do not to squirm or otherwise embarrass herself in front of her aunt and cousin, whom she was certain were watching her every move.

"It's good to see you again, sir." She strove to keep her voice carefully modulated.

"Lancaster," he repeated firmly. "I insist."

Her aunt gave a jarring cackle that made Rose jump. "When a man who owns as many guns as you do insists on something, who are we to argue?"

She and Anna Kate shared a hearty chuckle over her jest.

Rose was too busy reminding herself to breathe to join in. Sitting this close to Lancaster Tracy made him feel taller, broader, and infinitely more overpowering than he had during their earlier encounter.

Maybe it was the new gown that had her in such a tizzy. Maybe her petticoat was too tight. Or maybe she was more tired than she'd realized from her long journey west.

Though the kitchen staff served an enticing array of entrees, Rose was unable to work up the energy to dig in. She grew more weary by the second, until she was practically swaying in her seat.

Her aunt suddenly reached for her hand. "Are you well, dearest?"

"I am." Rose forced a smile. "Just a little tired, is all."

"Rupert." Aunt Winifred's voice was sharp.

Almost instantly, he appeared at her side. "You called, ma'am?"

"If you'll escort my youngest niece to her room and have refreshments sent to her."

Rose wilted with embarrassment. "You don't need to go to that sort of trouble on my account, ma'am."

"It's the least I can do, dearest." Her aunt's hand momentarily tightened on hers. "I've uprooted you from everything you've ever known to make this old woman happy in her dotage."

Rose swayed in her seat again. "I'm most grate—"

"Of course, you are." Her aunt waved away her words. "You have too much Monroe blood in you to be anything other than good to the bone." Her voice gentled. "Make sure you get plenty of rest. We need you in tiptop shape for your first shooting lesson in the morning."

Lancaster Tracy stood to assist Rose to her feet. "I very much look forward to your first lesson, Miss Addington."

"Rose," she corrected. "Just Rose." If they were dispensing with titles, she didn't want to be left out. "I look forward to our lesson, as well. Until then, I bid you good-night, sir."

"Lancaster," he reminded, lifting her hand to his lips and briefly pressing his mouth to her fingertips.

She nearly swooned at his callused touch and the brush of his whiskers against her skin. Fortunately, she'd already established the fact to both women who were watching them that she was physically exhausted. Hopefully, they would chalk up her shortness of breath to nothing more than that.

She was especially grateful for Rupert's arm to lean on as she made her exit. The occupants of the dining room must not have calculated how slow she was walking, because they resumed their conversation before she was out of earshot — a conversation in which she was the main attraction.

"This is difficult for her, isn't it?" Anna Kate's voice was hushed with concern.

"More than I ever imagined," Aunt Winifred sighed. "She's certainly not to blame for anything she has suffered. A more innocent soul I've never met."

Rupert's shoulders shook with silent mirth. "And they say eavesdroppers never hear anything good about themselves," he announced in a stage whisper.

Rose chuckled and leaned her head weakly against his shoulder while he finished escorting her to her room. "I reckon I have them all fooled," she joked.

"No, you don't, miss," he retorted gently. "I think your aunt has the right of it."

Chapter 5: Choices

Rose could hardly sleep due to the number of butterflies flitting around inside her stomach. As much as she was looking forward to seeing Lancaster Tracy again, part of her was deeply unsettled by the prospect.

Her aunt had prattled on and on all afternoon about the kind of beau she would be seeking for her youngest niece. He needed to be a "man of good breeding." As best as Rose could gather, that meant her future husband needed to come from a solid, well-established family — reputable, a real gentleman, and preferably a wealthy one.

"*Like the Morleys back in England,*" *her aunt had explained.*

"*Who are the Morleys?*" *she'd asked, feeling the first quickening of alarm in her chest.*

"*Mia Stanton's family. You haven't met them yet, but you will. Her father is an earl, and her brother is a viscount.*"

There was one major problem with her aunt's definition of an eligible bachelor. Lancaster Tracy would most likely not measure up to her standards. It was a pity, considering he was the first unmarried man in town Rose had met. And the handsomest. And the most charming.

He was so likable, too, and she could tell he liked her in return. If nothing else, though, they could be friends. She tried to content herself with that notion. However, her heart wasn't yet ready to remove him from her list of eligible bachelors.

Maybe I'm no better than my mother. Too strong-willed and determined to ever fit into a family like this.

Sighing, Rose rolled onto her side in bed and stared at the opposite wall. It was of no use. Sleep evaded her until the wee hours of the morning. She finally stole a few winks, but awoke with another radiating headache.

"Oh, dear!" She perched on the side of her bed with her head cradled in her hands.

A knock sounded on her door. Though it was soft, it still made her wince.

"It's me, miss. Davina."

"Do come in." It hurt Rose's head so much to raise her voice that she dropped it back into her hands with a groan.

"Rose," Davina hissed in distress. She quietly shut the door behind her and hurried across the room. "Are you well?"

"Migraine," Rose mumbled woefully. "And I need it to be gone, or I'll have to reschedule my first shooting lesson, along with my first round of dance and voice lessons this afternoon." She gave another rueful groan. Her aunt would probably have a fit over seeing her carefully planned schedule so thoroughly disrupted on the second day of her campaign to transform Rose into a belle of society.

"A headache is nothing to jest about, my dear. Do you get them often?" Davina came to stand beside her.

"Every day since my arrival in Texas." Maybe it was due to the change in climate. It was much drier here than it had been in Atlanta.

"May I?" Davina wiggled her strong, capable fingers at Rose. "Our mother taught me a little trick for soothing aching temples."

"By all means." Rose leaned her way. "Work your magic on this horrible beast."

"Close your eyes, and try to clear your mind." The cool pads of Davina's fingertips settled against Rose's temples and began to move in slow circles. "If I hit a sensitive spot, please say something, so I can adjust the pressure accordingly."

Beneath her careful ministrations, Rose's headache swiftly eased. By the time Davina's fingers finished moving, the pain had completely vanished. Rose lifted her head in amazement. "I don't know how to thank you."

"Your aunt pays me well," Davina reminded dryly.

"This is different," Rose insisted. "You were under no obligation to put my poor head out of its misery."

"Your friendship is more than enough," Davina assured, looking pleased. "Friends help each other, you know, without any expectation of payment in return."

"But—"

"But if you insist," Davina cut in merrily, "I wouldn't turn down a slice of apple pie if you happen to pass by the Cedar Falls Cafe."

Rose smiled at her. "One slice of apple pie is on its way!"

"Or two slices, if you want me to actually get a piece." Her maid rolled her eyes. "Clarice shares my weakness for Felipe's pies."

"Two slices of apple pie then," Rose chortled as Davina

helped her step once again into her new white and lavender gown. "Oh, my!" She stared at herself in the oval dressing mirror beside her wardrobe. "I think this dress grew lovelier overnight."

"As did the woman wearing it." Davina smoothed her hands over Rose's shoulders and picked a piece of lint from the rear scoop of her neckline. "I was worried you'd picked up a spot of something, but it came right off."

"Thank goodness!" Rose was anxious to live up to her aunt's expectations of turning her into a proper lady. "And thank you for your assistance again this morning." It would've taken her twice as long to dress on her own. A girl could easily grow accustomed to having others brush and style her hair, button her dresses, and help her look her best.

"Think nothing of it." Davina reached out to tweak her sleeve. "Now go learn how to shoot that nasty-looking pistol, so you can properly defend us the next time a snaggle-toothed farmer dares to invade our foyer."

To Rose's supreme agitation, Aunt Winifred abandoned her just outside the door of the gunsmith shop. "This is as far as I can go with you, dearest."

When Rose's lips parted in protest, her aunt silenced her with an upraised hand. "My man of business sent word that he's on his way back to town this morning. I'm meeting him at the cafe to discuss the new shipping route."

"Oh, Aunt Win," Rose implored. "I was so hoping we could enjoy our first shooting lesson together." She'd also been counting on her aunt to provide her normal vinegary buffer between her and her growing attraction to Lancaster Tracy.

"I am truly sorry, love." Her aunt glanced over her shoulder at Rupert, as if to ask him why he wasn't already wheeling her away. "But business comes before pleasure. Without it, there would be no funds for ladies' pistols or shooting lessons." She softened her lecture with a smile. "Mind you, there *is* a bit of a silver lining in my last-minute change of plans. My man of business will remain in town overnight, in which case he might be able to join us for dinner this evening. Blaine Eastman is an intelligent, successful, and highly accomplished gentleman. It would mean the world to me to have the pleasure of introducing you to him." She gave Rose a knowing smile. "He's from a big family in San Diego. Lawyers, every last one of them. And to top it all off, he's easy on the eyes."

Rose's heart sank at the realization that Jensen had been wrong about her aunt's man of business being a distant relative. Clearly, he was not. Even more concerning was the fact that her aunt appeared bent on pairing her off with a beau right away. She'd expected to be a little further along in her social training before that happened.

"I look forward to meeting him." She spoke mechanically through stiff lips. Little did her first potential beau know he was starting off with one serious disadvantage. He was not Lancaster Tracy.

"Not as much as I look forward to introducing the two of you. You'll get along famously." With that alarming prediction, her aunt signaled for Rupert to roll her down the street. Her gown of regal navy silk riffled in the breeze around her ankles. Despite her crippled state, she resembled a general heading into battle.

A jingle of a bell alerted Rose to the fact that Lancaster had opened the door of his shop for her. She glanced up at him, melting in pleasure beneath the admiring glint in his gaze. She could only hope he hadn't overheard too much of her aunt's discourse about Blaine Eastman.

"You look lovely this morning, Rose." He pushed the door wider and ushered her inside the building.

"Thank you, sir." The way he was looking at her made her feel pretty. He didn't look too shabby himself in a white dress shirt, black leather vest, and silver bolo. His head was uncovered this morning, revealing dark waves that tumbled across his forehead. A hint of auburn streaked them here and there. Her fingers itched to smooth one errant strand from his eyes.

You belong in a story of your own, Lancaster Tracy. The start of one was already swimming through her head, one in which he starred front and center.

"It sounds as if you'll be getting all spit and polished up this evening for another dinner engagement." Though his tone was nonchalant, his dark eyes probed hers speculatively.

Disappointment shivered through her at the realization that he'd overheard her aunt's announcement, after all. There was no point in denying it. "I'm afraid so. That is to say," she amended hastily, "my aunt's man of business sounds like a wonderful man. I look forward to meeting him." As soon as the words left her, she found herself hoping he didn't read too much into them.

"What's so wonderful about him?" Lancaster placed his hand on the small of her back to nudge her past the cash register. He led her to the adjoining room, which served as his firing range.

It was a long, narrow room. Paint lines on the floor divided it into three distinct shooting lanes. Each lane was approximately five feet in width. The paint lines continued to the far end of the room, where a round target stood at the base of each lane.

Rose shrugged helplessly, uncertain what the rugged gunsmith was hoping to hear. "According to my aunt, Mr. Eastman comes from a family of lawyers from San Diego. It sounds as if he serves her business interests in an exemplary manner. That is all I know, other than the fact that my aunt thinks he's handsome." She smiled ruefully. "As the old saying goes, beauty is in the eye of the beholder." She was withholding judgment until she met the man for herself. Removing her new pistol from her reticule, she held it in front of her, careful to keep the muzzle pointed down the lane and away from the two of them.

"Very good, Rose." Lancaster's voice was infused with approval. "You remembered what I said about treating every gun like it's loaded, even when it's not."

"I promised I would." She gripped the gun more firmly. "Lesson number one successfully mastered, sir!" She gave him a mock salute with her free hand.

When he reached for her weapon, she handed it to him without question, trying not to shiver when their fingers brushed during the handoff. Every instinct in her shouted that he'd done it on purpose. He was flirting with her.

And I am letting him.

He swiftly loaded the cartridges in the cylinder. "If you don't mind me asking, Rose, what attributes are you seeking in a beau, since your aunt clearly intends for you to have one?"

Though she *did* mind him asking about her aunt's less than subtle plans for her future, she answered him as honestly as she could. "A man of character and impeccable integrity." Her next breath felt a trifle shaky. "Like my father was," she added in a softer voice.

"I'm sorry for your loss, Rose." Lancaster looked inordinately pleased by her answer. "You've yet to address me as Lancaster, by the way. Why is that?"

She shook her head, feeling suddenly shy. She didn't know how to answer his question. It felt so loaded. So personal. So intimate.

"Or Lan," he added in a teasing voice, "if Lancaster is too long a handle for you."

If she'd harbored any doubts before, he was most definitely flirting with her. She hid a smile as she silently rolled the shorter version of his name across her tongue. *Lan.* "I like it," she confessed. *And you,* she added inside her head. She wasn't sure what it was about him that interested her so much. She'd never experienced this level of awareness around a man before. It was both exhilarating and unsettling.

"I'm glad you like it since I'm stuck with it." He gave a husky chuckle. "And it hasn't escaped me that you've yet to answer my question."

"I don't know how to answer it...Lan." Her heart raced as she experimented with calling him by his name for the first time. And not just his first name, the shortened version of it, which felt even more intimate. "I reckon it's because we only met yesterday."

"True, but I'm already looking forward to getting to know you better, Rose. A lot better." He handed her weapon back with the barrel facing the floor.

"I look forward to that, too, sir...er, Lan," she corrected.

"Does my plain speaking make you nervous?" He studied her intently.

"A little," she admitted breathlessly.

"That's better than indifference. If it makes you feel any

better, I'm less comfortable around you in your new dress than I was in your old dress."

She stared at him in amazement. "How is that supposed to make me feel better?"

"I don't know." He crinkled the corners of his eyes at her.

"To be frank," she informed him wryly, "I'm less comfortable in my new dress than I was in my old dress."

He looked intrigued. "Why?"

"I could ask you the same thing," she retorted without thinking, then immediately wanted to bite her tongue for being so bold.

He smirked. "That's easy. If you get too high class on me, you'll be too uppity to court a lowly gunsmith."

She drew a sharp breath. "Lan!"

He snorted out a laugh. "Oh, come on, Rose! I believe I've made my interest in you clear."

She glanced away from him. "I-I'm not certain my aunt will approve."

He was silent for a moment. "No offense, but I'm far more interested in what you think of me."

Though her heart felt like it was pounding a thousand beats per minute, she forced her gaze back to his. "I'm still forming my opinion of you." It was the most honest answer she could give at the moment.

"Fair enough." He didn't look the least bit disturbed by her honesty.

"So far, it's a good one," she continued in a thready voice.

"Then I shall strive to make it a better one." He winked at her. "It might help if you share a bit more about what you're searching for in a beau."

"To be honest, I haven't been searching at all," she confessed. "Not while I lived in Atlanta, at any rate. I was mostly just surviving." She hesitated before adding, "In a poorhouse." She watched closely for his reaction.

There was no judgment in his expression, only concern. "Dare I ask what you were doing in a poorhouse?"

"I was poor," she supplied with a smile.

He cocked his head at her, still looking concerned. "That's not what I meant."

"I was orphaned after the war." She waved a hand. "It's a common story in Atlanta. I was fortunate to find a job. To have a roof over my head and food in my belly. And to make some new friends along the way. This..." She waved a hand at her expensive new gown. "This is going to take some getting used to. It's not me, Lan. It might never be me. If that changes your opinion of—"

"It doesn't," he cut in flatly.

She faced him, drawing short, shallow breaths. "There are things you don't know about me, Lancaster Tracy. Things my aunt doesn't yet know about me." If her aunt found out about the manuscript she'd hidden in her bedroom, it might be enough to get her pitched right back into the street.

"Like I said earlier," he jutted his chin at her, "I look forward to getting to know you better. Something tells me your secrets will be worth knowing when you decide to trust me with them."

"When?" She chuckled airily. "That's a very big assumption, sir."

"Lancaster," he corrected automatically. "And having faith isn't the same thing as being presumptuous, Rose. I trust you know the difference?" He raised his eyebrows in challenge at her.

She shook her head in bemusement. "Since my humble beginnings appear to fascinate you, I regret to inform you that my story is a rather uninteresting one."

He didn't so much as blink. "I'd prefer to be the judge of that."

If he was anything, he was persistent. She couldn't help admiring that about him. "Then I'll give you the short version. Once my father passed, I thought I was alone in the world. At the time, I was unaware I had an aunt out west. She did know, however, and took it upon herself to seek me out." She spread her hands. "And here I am."

"And here you are." He searched her gaze for a moment, before stepping behind her to lightly cradle her hands between his. He helped her raise and aim the pistol. "Hold her steady, remove the safety, and cock it by pulling back on the hammer. Like this." He pressed his thumb over her thumb to guide the small lever back. It clicked into place. "Now pull the trigger, Rose." His voice was low and rumbly in her ear, stirring her emotions to reckless levels.

She closed her eyes and squeezed the trigger. The sharp crack of the bullet as it released from the barrel made her jump. "That was louder than I expected." Her ears were ringing. Her headache from earlier returned at a lurking intensity — not a full-blown ache, but enough to make her aware of its presence.

"That's nothing compared to some of the hunting rifles I have in stock." His forehead wrinkled contemplatively as he stepped around her to study her expression. "But if it bothers you, I can fetch some cotton for your ears."

"Yes, please." She laid her weapon on a low shelf resting between her and the firing lane. "I'd rather not cut our lesson short due to the return of my silly migraine. My maids have made it clear they are depending on me to defend them from all future dusty intruders."

Lancaster curled his upper lip at her. "Your maids, eh? That rolled off your tongue easily enough. You might be adjusting to your new, more sumptuous lifestyle quicker than you expected."

She stared at him, wondering why he sounded so accusing all of a sudden. She hoped it was nothing more than her imagination. "Believe me, there's no hardship adjusting to a warm bath and three meals per day." In time, she would probably adjust to her new wardrobe, as well. She could only hope and pray it would be as easy to bow to her aunt's wishes to secure an advantageous marriage. Up until she'd met Lancaster Tracy, it hadn't entered her mind to question her aunt's wishes on the topic. She was certainly doing so now.

"I don't reckon your aunt expects anything in return for her outpouring of generosity?" He moved to the other side of the room and returned with some cotton. He dropped it into her palm.

"I agreed to serve as her personal secretary and companion, but..." *I haven't yet gotten started on either of those things.* It was puzzling the way her Aunt Win's attentions seemed to be focused so singularly on her launch into society. She'd not so much as broached the subject of putting Rose to work yet.

"There's always a but, isn't there?" Lancaster's voice adopted a sardonic note.

"My aunt has been all that is kind," Rose assured him. "I don't wish to sound ungrateful in any way." She had no idea why she was speaking her mind so freely to a man she barely knew. Nevertheless, it was a relief to unburden herself a little. "Part of me feels guilty, though, that all I've done so far is allow her to purchase an exorbitant number of new dresses for me. She's also paying for dancing, voice, and pianoforte lessons. Though I have no complaints about any of those things, I'm not accustomed to doing all the taking without giving anything in return. In the past, I've always earned my keep."

"Naturally, your aunt is grooming you for marriage." The bitterness in Lancaster's voice ratcheted upward.

By summer's end, yes. Rose was trying not to think about it too hard. "You say that like it's a bad thing." She shot him a puzzled look as she placed the cotton in her ears. "It's what girls do. We grow up. We get married. We start families of our own." She reached for the weapon he'd reloaded for her. Shrugging away his assistance, she fired the remaining rounds in quick succession, hitting the target with all except one of the bullets.

Lancaster's gaze was glowing with approval by the time she laid down her weapon a second time. "Is that what you wish for, Rose?"

"For a family of my own?" She was surprised by his persistence in keeping the conversation going. "I have nothing against the institution of marriage, if that's what you're asking. Why should I?"

"But is it what you wish for?" he pressed. "Or is there something else you want more?" There was an oddly urgent tenor to his question that told her that her answer mattered to him.

She shrugged and jimmied with her gun in an attempt to reload it herself. "I think it would be a very different world if young men and women got what they wished for, which they generally do not." If she could have anything she wanted, she'd choose to become a published author, but she was all too aware of how unlikely that was, now or ever.

"But if you *could* have what you wished for, Rose, what would it be?" Lancaster set a partially full box of ammunition on the shelf in front of her, silently demonstrating how to load the first bullet. Then he handed back her weapon so she could finish loading it beneath his watchful eye.

She peeked at him from beneath her lashes, unable to resist teasing him. "What would you say if I told you I wished more than anything to marry?"

He was silent for several moments. When he finally spoke, he sounded disappointed. "I might be tempted to accuse you of not being entirely truthful."

Rose gave an unladylike snicker. "You remind me of a hunting dog with a juicy bone, Lancaster Tracy." She finished reloading the revolver and spun the cylinder. "Very well." She shot off the first bullet. "There is something else I want, but it's mine and mine alone." She shot the second bullet. "It's not something I've shared with my aunt, because I doubt she will approve. And I'm most certainly not going to share it with a man I just met." *There!* He could think whatever he wanted about that, but he deserved the set-down for prying into things that didn't concern him. She fired the last three bullets and blew tauntingly at the smoke that curled up from the barrel.

"Then earning your confidence will become my sole focus, starting now." His cocky smile was back as he reached for her revolver. He opened the cylinder and eyed the empty compartment.

She narrowed her gaze at him. "You watched me shoot all five bullets, so what are you looking for?"

"People lose count all the time, Rose, so it's very important to check for stray bullets before storing your weapon." He clapped the cylinder shut. "Lesson number one, remember?"

She hadn't forgotten. Rolling her eyes at him, she recited, "Every weapon is loaded even when it's not, Mr. Gunsmith."

"Always and forever, Rose. Always and forever."

There was a caressing edge to his words that made her wonder if they were still speaking about revolvers.

Or something else entirely.

Chapter 6: Divided Loyalties
Lancaster

One month later

Lancaster had never enjoyed a set of shooting lessons more than the ones he gave to Rose Marie Addington. It was way too bad she was related to the owners of the vast Monroe shipping conglomerate. Though her aunt's wealth and social aspirations represented everything he abhorred and had so willingly left behind in Boston, he found himself drawn to Rose in ways that even he could not explain.

She was different from the debutantes he'd danced with back east. Despite her elegant new wardrobe, there was no artifice in her. No secret agendas. She was intelligent, witty, and kindhearted to everyone she encountered. The townsfolk, who'd never hesitated to whisper and poke fun at her aunt's many eccentricities, were just as quick to lather the woman's niece with unadulterated approval. She was adored by everyone from the smallest tots hiding behind their mothers' skirts to Jensen Atkinson, one of the oldest fellows in town.

The only item she continuously refused to be forth-coming about was the secret she'd alluded to during her first shooting lesson. It was just as important to her as the marriage her aunt was working so hard to procure for her. So far, though, he'd been unsuccessful in wrangling the secret from her.

Fortunately, it was Monday, which meant her next lesson would begin in a matter of minutes. He couldn't wait to wear her down a little more on the topic. Maybe, just maybe, today would be the day she finally revealed her secret to him.

Rose breezed into his shop at eight o'clock sharp in yet another new gown. The pale pink silk made his heart sink. With each passing day, she looked a little less like the half-wilted Rose who'd first rolled into town on the seat of Jensen's delivery wagon. Her faded blue dress had been replaced by mountains of lace, ruffles, and other fineries. Her shy and weary wistfulness had been replaced by a veneer of newfound poise and confidence.

"Another new dress, eh?" He made no attempt to hide the grumble in his voice.

"Yes. Aunt Win insisted." She sounded rueful. "If she keeps this up, she's going to have to add on another room to her home to hold my ever-growing wardrobe. I told her that, too, but all she did was give me one of her do-not-cross-me looks. Apparently, I'm on a mission to try out a few more dresses before the barn raising coming in September. Are you going, by the way?"

"Everybody's going." Though he didn't like the changes in Rose's appearance, he could tell she genuinely appreci-ated everything her aunt was doing for her. Somehow, she'd managed not to let it completely spoil her.

"Are you taking anyone special with you?" Rose glanced

out the front window of his shop, looking utterly engrossed in whatever was taking place outside.

He followed her gaze, but saw nothing unusual, just ol' Jensen chugging past in his delivery wagon. Felipe flew down the sidewalk after him with one of his covered pies in hand.

"I'll be swinging a hammer like the rest of the menfolk." His gut told him that wasn't what she was truly asking. "I haven't yet decided if I'm staying for the dance and picnic afterward. Why?" He waited until she turned her shy gaze back in his direction. "Are you angling for a well-armed escort, Rose?" He didn't enjoy large social gatherings, but he did like the idea of spinning Rose out on the dance floor for the first time.

She flushed and shook her head. "My aunt's man of business, Blaine, will be in town, again. He's already asked to escort me." She gave her new dress a twirl in the center of the shop. Her skirts ballooned outward, making her chuckle. "Do you like my dress?"

You're on a first name basis with Blaine Eastman now? He gnashed his teeth in irritation. "It's lovely." He turned his back on her while he fetched a fresh box of ammunition from his main display case.

"You don't sound like you do," she teased, giving the dress another twirl. "And to think the Beaumont sisters worked so hard on it."

"Why does it matter what I think of it?" he groused. "Seeing as you're going to the dance with someone else?"

"Why, Lancaster Tracy!" Her slender hands settled on her hips. "I don't recall you asking me to go with you."

"I did a few minutes ago." He slapped the box of ammunition on the counter between them. "And you turned me down flat."

"You most certainly did not!" Her chin came up. "You more or less accused me of needing a protector, despite all the shooting lessons you've given me. Not that it would've made any difference if you had invited me. My aunt would never approve of—" She bit down on her lower lip, flushing deeply as she whirled away from him.

What? His jaw dropped. "Are you trying to say she disapproves of me?" *Me? Even though I meet every one of her ridiculous requirements in a beau for her precious niece?* Neither Winifred Monroe nor Rose knew that, of course. He'd been careful to continue playing the part of a country gunsmith in front of them. They had no idea he had all the social spit and polish they were looking for, along with a big family name and a trust fund to go with it — money he hadn't touched in over five years.

"She did not say that precisely." Rose's voice reverberated with misery as she retreated to the far side of the room to stare at a rack of rifles. "It was unforgivable of me to even imply such a thing, though I hope you will, in fact, forgive me."

Unfortunately, her pleading for grace did not erase the ache in his heart brought on by her revelation.

"Say something, Lan." Her voice shook.

Oh, he had plenty to say, but he intended to look her in the eye when he did. He stomped to the front door, locked it, and reached up to turn the *Open* sign to *Closed*. "Very well. Let's talk. Not in here, though. In private." He waited until she turned around to jerk his head in the direction of the shooting range.

She nodded, white-faced, and followed him. "I'm so sorry," she breathed in a voice barely above a whisper. "If I could take back what I said, I would."

"I'm not sorry." He turned to face her with his arms

crossed over his chest. "We've been working our way toward this conversation for weeks."

"I-I don't know what you mean." She strolled around him to the center firing lane. It was her favorite lane. She lifted her slender arms and took aim at the target, pretending like she was holding a weapon.

He strode across the room to stand behind her. "I think you do, Rose. You've allowed me to court you in my own way for the past month, and now you're pushing me away. I think I deserve to know why."

"You consider this to be courting?" She whirled around to face him. "I've done nothing more than faithfully attend my shooting lessons."

Her movements brought them closer, stirring a fresh layer of tension between them.

"Lessons which I normally charge for and finish in three thirty-minute sessions," he retorted evenly. "It's written clearly on the poster in my front window and on every other piece of paper floating around my shop."

"Lan," she squeaked, looking uncertain. "We really shouldn't be having this conversation. It's not in any way appropriate."

"What isn't appropriate?" They were alone. As far as he was concerned, that meant they could afford to be bluntly honest with each other. "The fact that I care about you, or the fact that you care about me in return?"

Her pale cheeks bloomed with color. "Please don't, Lan. You're raising a mess of questions I don't know how to even begin to answer."

"How about we just cut straight to the point, then?" He glared at her. "You've been quietly falling for a man your aunt doesn't approve of, while enduring the beginning stages of courtship with a man of her choosing — one you do not and never will love."

Rose's blue-green gaze became luminous with unshed tears. "Oh, Lan!" She reached blindly for him. "What are we going to do?"

He caught his breath roughly. Not once, in all of his daydreams, had he pictured her admitting the truth so quickly. He should've known better, though. She was Rose, for crying out loud! The one woman in the world who'd managed to steal his heart right out from beneath his nose. He couldn't have stopped her if he'd tried. It was one of those things there was no going back on.

He drew her closer, wrapping his arms around her like he'd longed to do for the past month. "What we're going to do about it is this." He bent his head to claim her lips.

She sighed and melted into his embrace.

He cuddled her closer, deepening their kiss and glorying in her sweet surrender. He was so lost in her arms that it was laughable. He could've kept on kissing her forever, but there were still so many things they needed to discuss. So many important concerns yet to work out between them. It was with the greatest reluctance that he broke off their kiss to search her beautiful eyes. He silently begged her to search his in return and, by some miracle, interpret at least some of what was on his heart.

"Lan." She touched his cheek, looking utterly stunned.

He turned his head to kiss her fingers. "In case I haven't made myself clear, I love you, Rose."

"You're right, Lan. I knew it. Deep inside, I knew something was happening between us. It was just easier to pretend that it wasn't."

It wasn't the declaration of love he'd hoped for in return, but it was close enough. For now. He nuzzled her temple, breathing in her clean, flowery scent. He'd become addicted to it in recent days.

"Because of your aunt?" he prodded when she fell silent.

"Yes." She gave him a sad smile. "I didn't need another secret to keep from her."

He tensed at her reference to the one thing she'd been keeping from him all this time. "Your secrets are mine to protect now. You know that, right?"

She raised herself to her tiptoes to brush her lips against his again. "You are mine to protect now, too, Lan."

He grew still, wondering if she meant what he thought she meant.

"I love you, too, Lan," she confessed softly against his lips. "You were right about that, as well."

The last walls in his heart crumbled at her feet. A man could survive for a very long time on words like that. He kissed her slowly and tenderly. "Are you going to make me beg to learn your other secret?"

"As tempting as it sounds? No." She glanced away from him, looking uncertain.

He drew a heavy breath. "If your intention is to torture me, you're doing a very fine job of it."

She tipped her flaming face up to his. "I write love stories, Lan. There! Now you know." As if unable to bear his scrutiny a moment longer, she buried her face against his chest.

Unbelievable! He kissed the top of her head, utterly entranced by what he'd learned about her. *I'm going to marry an author.* He couldn't have been more tickled. Or proud. He'd always assumed her secret would be worth the wait. Something unique and special, just like her, and he was right.

"Aren't you going to say something?" Her voice was muffled against the front of his leather vest.

He kissed the top of her head again. "You're an amazingly talented woman, Rose Marie Addington. That you are."

She raised her head. "That's it? You're not completely scandalized?"

He gave her an incredulous look. "Darling, I'm a gunsmith, not a monk."

A smile played at the edges of her mouth.

"Have you submitted anything for publication yet?" He was dying to know more about her secret — how she'd gotten started and how long she'd been writing.

"I want to," she sighed. "I want to so badly, but there hasn't been any opportunity since I moved to Cedar Falls. My aunt keeps me running to teas, luncheons, and parties. I fall exhausted into bed every night, wishing more than anything for the time to finish copying my manuscript at long last."

"You've already written it?" That was news to him. She'd given him no clue up to this point as to where she was in the process.

"Written and revised it too many times to count. That's why I need to create a clean copy before submitting it. However, my aunt has made so many disparaging statements about the *scandalous drivel* young women read nowadays, that I don't dare pull it out to work on until after dark each night."

"You're welcome to use my shop," he offered. "We can shorten your shooting lesson to give you as much time as you need to get a clean copy of your manuscript written up."

"What a marvelous idea, Lan!" Awe stained her gaze. "You would really do that for me?"

"I would do anything for you." He spun her in a short jig. "Dance with you. Court you. Even marry you someday." He dipped her low over his arm. "When you're ready."

Her cheeks paled again. "Lan," she moaned when he stood her upright again. "I wasn't jesting about my aunt's disapproval. She has some very specific ideas about the sort of man she intends for me to marry."

"None of that matters any longer." He lightly tapped the tip of her nose. "I love you, and you love me. That's what matters."

"I do love you," she sighed. "But my aunt's opinion still counts with me."

"Because of the lifestyle she is able to provide you?" It was a cruel question, but he had to know the truth.

Rose sniffed in disdain. "You do recall that I spent nearly a year in the poorhouse?"

His heart twisted at the memory. "I'm sorry for what you suffered, Rose." He wasn't sorry, however, for the honest and decent woman it had turned her into.

"My aunt's good opinion matters to me, Lan, because she's all the family I have left. After the many years we spent estranged, I don't wish to lose her again."

His heart sank at her words.

"I don't wish to lose you, either," she added in a choked voice. "Do you see the conundrum I find myself in?"

Relief flooded his chest. "Then there's only one thing left for us to do." He drew a finger down the side of her face. "I'll just have to convince your aunt that I'm worthy of you."

"What if we're unable to change her mind about the plans she's already spinning for my future?" Rose raised anxious eyes to his.

He shook his head in disgust. "There's no way I'm going to stand by and do nothing while she marries you off to that stuffed shirt man of business of hers."

A nervous chuckle escaped the woman in his arms. "He never stood a chance with me, Lan," she confessed in a breathy voice. "Not after I met you."

His heart sang at her words. "Then it's settled, Rose. When the time is right, I'm going to ask you to marry me, and you're going to say yes."

Her gaze glowed into his. "You're the cockiest gunsmith I've ever met."

His chest swelled. "While we're on the topic of my many imperfections, I might as well do a little more bragging." He tightened his arms around her. "Be assured I can afford to keep my wife in style, more so than every pompous toad your aunt has paraded past you during the last month."

She giggled and twined her arms around his neck. "I already own enough dresses to last me a lifetime, Lan."

He seriously doubted that, but he adored her humble attitude and contented spirit. They were rare treasures, indeed. He nuzzled her temple again. "It's settled, then. You'll continue courting me in secret, while I work on convincing your aunt I'm the right man for her beloved niece."

Rose bit her lower lip. "Yes, I'll continue courting you in private, Lan, but I honestly don't know what it'll take to convince my aunt we are right for each other." She looked distressed. "Or if such a thing is even possible."

He ducked his head to bring them eye-to-eye. "Do you trust me, Rose?"

She nodded, looking anxious. "I told you my deepest, darkest secret, didn't I?"

Guilt gnawed at his gut at the knowledge that he'd yet

to reveal his own deepest secrets to her. However, keeping his secrets from her had been the only way of determining that Rose was capable of loving him. *Him*. Not his family name. Not his wealth. She loved the man he truly was. The bounty hunter turned gunsmith, with calluses on his hands and scars she didn't yet know about from one close shave during a particularly harrowing bounty collection.

His jaw tightened in determination. "Then believe me when I say this, darling. I *will* earn your aunt's regard, and she *will* give us her blessing. You can take that to the bank."

"I believe you, Lan." Rose's heart shone in her eyes as she gave him her word. "Thank you for your willingness to do whatever it takes to win my aunt over, because I don't ever want to have to make the choice my mother did. She chose love over family, and it nearly destroyed her. Though I would do the same if it came to that," she shivered at the thought, "I'd rather have both, Lan. So that's exactly what I'll be praying for, night and day, until we succeed in our mission."

He drew her close for another tender kiss. The knowledge that she would choose love if she had to was more than enough for him. He intended to do everything in his power to ensure she never had to make the same horrible choice her mother had been forced to make.

Or that I was forced to make.

He loved Rose too much. He wanted better for her. Far better. If it were possible, he'd give her the world.

Chapter 7: Armed and Dangerous

Rose

It took no less than five more shooting lessons for Rose to sneak her entire manuscript to Lancaster's shop. She carried the sections of her manuscript in the largest reticule she owned. As promised, he allotted most of their sessions to allowing her to work quietly and alone on the newest copy of her manuscript. Instead of relegating her to a shooting gallery smelling of gunpowder, he emptied out a storage closet and furnished it with a small desk, chair, and lamp. That way she could work in true solitude, out of sight from the curious eyes of any customer or passer-by who might pop their head into the shooting gallery.

By the time August rolled around, she was nearly finished with the project. All that remained was her book dedication and the final scene of her story, which she was retooling for the umpteenth time. She felt like skipping instead of walking to her Wednesday morning shooting lesson.

Her steps slowed as she neared the gunsmith shop. An unfamiliar sight awaited her, one that made her catch her breath. Lancaster had installed a whole row of blue porcelain urns on the front porch of his shop, five in all. They were blooming with wild roses in every hue — white, red, yellow, pink, and orange.

"Not so subtle," she whispered as she traversed the porch and reached for the door handle. It was a sweetly romantic gesture, nonetheless. She couldn't wait to tell him so!

The moment she stepped inside his shop, she realized their next kiss would have to wait. She additionally realized that her morning would not be going as originally planned.

Blaine Eastman was standing in the entryway, facing the door as if he'd been waiting for someone.

Me. Her heart skipped a beat, and not in a good way. What was he doing here? It didn't feel like happenstance.

His black hair was slicked back with the pomade he was so fond of, and he was wearing one of his nattiest plaid suits. His shoes were polished to a full gloss, and silver cufflinks winked from the wrists of his white dress shirt. He looked far too suave and sophisticated for a small town like Cedar Falls. Rose much preferred the leather vests and Stetsons that her favorite gunsmith wore.

As if reading her thoughts, Lan caught her eye from behind his cash register and gave her a knowing smirk. "Good morning, Miss Addington. Are you ready for your next lesson?" His use of her last name instead of her first name felt like a warning.

Before she could respond, Blaine stepped between them with his hands outstretched. "There you are, my dear. I was hoping to see you this morning before I left town."

My dear? She was most certainly *not* his dear. "I thought you'd already left town." She wrinkled her nose as she endured the cold kiss he pressed to the back of her hand.

"As if I would leave without saying goodbye to you," he scoffed. "I'll be departing shortly, but I wanted to assure you I'll be back in time to escort you to the barn raising as promised."

She was at a loss for what to say since she'd not precisely accepted his invitation to attend the barn raising with him. On the contrary, she'd been purposefully avoiding giving him an answer. She'd been too worried about offending her aunt. In hindsight, dragging her heels on the subject had been a mistake.

Blaine smiled broadly at her, as if confident she wouldn't contradict him. "So this is where you come for your shooting lessons." He spun around with her to face Lancaster, while keeping one hand resting beneath her elbow. "For two months straight. You must be a poor pupil indeed, my dear, to require so much additional assistance."

Her face burned with mortification. "I've never owned a gun before," she admitted in the hopes that her answer would satisfy his curiosity. "There's been a lot to learn."

"I'd be more than happy to continue your lessons myself upon my return." His hand on her elbow tightened, making her glance up in concern to determine what was amiss. She found him studying Lancaster with a hard, angry expression.

"If you gentlemen will excuse me." She wiggled her shoulders and took a step forward in an attempt to escape his grasp. "I have a dance lesson to attend shortly. I must be on my way."

"So soon?" Blaine dropped his hand from her elbow to study her with chilly amusement. "What about your shooting lesson?"

"It'll have to wait." The look in his eyes was unsettling. She couldn't wait to be rid of his snide and presumptuous presence for the next month. "As it stands, I got a later start than I intended this morning. Please accept my apologies, Mr. Tracy." She caught Lan's eye, begging him to understand the necessity for her hasty departure. Something about Blaine's demeanor felt a bit creepy this morning. "I promise to work twice as hard during our next lesson."

"I have no doubt you will," he assured blandly.

"I'm heading in the same direction." Blaine crooked an arm at her. "I'd be happy to escort you home."

I'd much rather you didn't. It was all she could do not to recoil a step back. "Oh, that won't be necessary. It isn't far at all," she protested, tucking the strap of her reticule more firmly against her shoulder. "I need to make a stop at the dressmakers along the way."

"I don't mind the detour," he assured smoothly. Too smoothly.

Lancaster, who'd been fiddling with something behind his cash register, stepped around the counter to give Rose his most courtly bow. "You've done well in your lessons, m'lady." He reached for her hand and lightly kissed the top of it. "So well, in fact, that I might soon be forced to recommend your matriculation to your aunt." His tone was teasing, but his expression was deadly serious.

It sounded alarmingly like he was planning to end their shooting lessons altogether, which made no sense. What about her manuscript? She was so close to finishing it. She couldn't stop now.

"Thank you, sir." Her heart sped like it always did at his touch. She searched his gaze, sensing something was wrong. "I will be forever grateful to you for teaching me how to defend myself."

He grimaced instead of looking pleased. As he straightened, he lost his balance and bumped smartly into her.

Blaine gave a low snicker that he quickly covered with a cough.

She gasped in surprise. "Are you well, sir?"

"Pardon my lack of grace," Lancaster muttered, shuffling back a step.

She eyed him with concern. Something was most definitely wrong.

"I have one last request before you go." He raised his gaze to hers and held it, despite his unsteadiness on his feet. "Recite lesson one for me again."

"Every gun is loaded," she complied in a breathless voice, wondering why it was so important that she repeat it to him in front of Blaine Eastman.

"Yes, they are." His jaw clenched. "Every last gun is loaded, Miss Addington. Never forget it." With a grim nod of dismissal, he pivoted away from them and returned to his vigil behind the cash register.

As Blaine took her arm and led her from the shop, she glanced over her shoulder at Lancaster. His dark gaze burned into hers with a message she couldn't interpret. It wasn't simply jealousy. She wished she knew what he was thinking.

Her own thoughts were in a muddle as she stepped outside.

What did I do wrong? Surely Lan doesn't believe I'm being unfaithful to him! With Blaine Eastman, of all people! She could barely tolerate the man's presence.

She was so caught up in her fretting that she didn't immediately notice her escort was leading her in the opposite direction of the dressmaker's shop. When she finally realized his error, her steps slowed. *Good gracious!* She blinked at the scenery around them. They were well on their way to the opposite side of town, past both the mayor's office and boarding house.

Blaine shot her a harried look and picked up his pace, all but dragging her along the sidewalk beside him.

"We've gone too far, sir!" She attempted to tug her hand free. "We must turn around at once."

He clamped his other hand over hers, anchoring it to his arm like a vise. "Be patient, my dear. Your dance instructor has something special planned for you this morning. Please forgive me for divulging that bit of information. From what I understand, it was intended to be a surprise."

"Mr. Roth is planning a surprise for me?" That didn't sound the least bit like the gaunt-faced, uninteresting dance instructor who walked her through the same dull routine during each of her weekly lessons.

"Indeed he is. That's the real reason your aunt sent me to fetch you from the gunsmith's shop."

The knowledge that her aunt was in on the surprise should've made her feel better, but it didn't. Something felt terribly off about the entire ordeal.

Blaine used her momentary distraction to steer her into an alley between two boarded up warehouses.

Fear spurted through Rose. *This is wrong. This is all wrong!* "No," she gasped, yanking on her arm with all of her might. Blaine Eastman was out of his mind if he thought she was going to blindly follow him to a remote section of town without a better explanation than the one he'd given her so far.

He didn't answer.

"Stop," she begged piteously. "I need a moment to catch my breath."

Blaine continued to ignore her, increasing their pace again.

Her alarm intensified. *I have to get away from him!* Her lips parted as she sucked in a breath to scream.

He clapped a hand over her mouth. "Keep quiet," he growled.

Warbling out a protest, she writhed beneath his grasp, but he quickly overpowered her.

A few feet ahead of them, a metal door opened to the warehouse on their right, and a shadowy figure stepped out. He was dressed in solid black. Even the mask covering his face was black.

Rose frenziedly renewed her struggles, but Blaine dragged her through the doorway as if she weighed no more than a fly. The masked man clanged the heavy door shut behind them.

She found herself inside an enormous room, lit only by the faint rays of sunlight filtering through a few broken, dirt-encrusted windows. Dozens of crates were stacked haphazardly around them. The walls were drenched in cobwebs, and a thick layer of dust covered the floor. It was clear the place hadn't seen much use in a while. Not the legal kind, at any rate.

Why did they bring me here? Her heart shuddered with dread as her overactive imagination kicked into high gear, spewing out one nightmarish reason after another.

The shadowy figure pulled off his mask and beheld her with pity.

It was Mr. Roth. Rose's terrified gaze swung between her dance instructor and her aunt's man of business. *This was her surprise?* Unless she was back at home, caught up in a very bad dream, she could only come up with one logical explanation for what was happening. The two dastardly men had conspired to kidnap her!

"Please forgive me, Miss Rose," Mr. Roth babbled,

pulling off one of his gloves to run a hand through his dark, thinning hair. "I regret it had to come to this. Believe me, if there was any other way—"

"Enough," Blaine snarled. "There *was* another way, you fool, but you failed to help me bring it to fruition!" He dumped Rose unceremoniously into a rickety wooden chair in the center of the room. It creaked and wobbled, but it held her weight. "Tie her up!"

"You blame me?" her dance instructor squeaked. His pale features scrunched with incredulity, making Rose think of a quivering rat. "I did my part, and it wasn't easy. I have no experience whatsoever in giving dance lessons to privileged young debutantes."

Privileged? Rose sniffed in disgust. Apparently, the cad had no idea just how humble her background was. "Well, that explains a lot," she muttered beneath her breath. No wonder the man had proven to be such an uninspired instructor. He was nothing more than a henchman to a vile criminal.

She still had no idea what she'd done to provoke Blaine Eastman into attempting something so dastardly. Only yesterday, he'd broken bread with her family at her aunt's dinner table. He'd pretended to be their friend. Had he been pretending all along? Was he even a real attorney?

Blaine slid a six-shooter from the pocket of his trousers and trained it on her. "Go on and tie her up, Mr. Roth. I have a ransom note to deliver, and time's a-wasting."

A ransom note? Rose's eyes widened in horror. So *that's* what this was about! She watched in disbelief as Mr. Roth pulled a coil of rope from inside his suit jacket.

"Blaine," she pleaded softly. "You don't have to do this."

"You left me no choice." His lips twisted. "If you'd have given me any hope whatsoever of returning my affections, I wouldn't have had to resort to such drastic measures." He gnashed his teeth. "But you didn't. I had my suspicions as to why, but I only just this morning confirmed them." He took a menacing step closer to her. "A lowly gunsmith, Rose? I think we both know your aunt will never approve of him."

Indignation burned in her. "At least he's a real gunsmith," she spat, sorely doubting that the man standing in front of her possessed half the credentials he claimed. "He's a better man than you!"

"You have no idea what you're talking about!" A vein ticked in his neck. "My family has served your family for three generations," he sneered.

Her mind raced. "Perhaps your father did and his father before him. But you?" She shook her head piteously. "Something tells me you've never had my aunt's best interest in mind." It was unfortunate that the offspring of her aunt's last man of business had turned out to be such a scoundrel. Even more surprising was how easily Blaine had managed to pull the wool over everyone's eyes. Winifred Monroe wasn't normally so gullible.

As the truth sank home, Rose began to tremble. "This is my fault," Rose whispered in horror. Her aunt had been so caught up in righting past wrongs with her long-lost niece that she'd become vulnerable to the wiles of Blaine Eastman. The son of her former man of business. Someone she'd undoubtedly trusted by association alone.

"At last, we agree on something." Blaine lifted his gun to point it directly between her eyes. "In a town with so few eligible bachelors, sweeping you off your feet should've been a much easier task. Sadly, you let your dirt-poor roots bleed through and take over."

Rose glared back at him. "You say that like you're any better," she seethed. The fact that he could stand there holding a gun on her and still act so self-righteous was beyond her comprehension.

Blaine cocked his weapon. The clicking sound echoed ominously through the near-empty warehouse.

Mr. Roth sprang between them like a wiry chicken and hastily started tying her hands behind the chair. Her feet were next. She managed to kick him so hard in the chest that she nearly upturned the chair. His bony hands fumbled so badly with the ropes afterward that it took him several tries to secure them.

If he'd been her only assailant, she might've stood a chance. However, Blaine stood over them the entire time with a weapon she no longer doubted he would use on her, given the right provocation.

After she was securely tied, he shook his head in disgust and pocketed his gun. He stalked toward the door and paused with his hand on the knob, half-turning back in their direction. "Keep her quiet. If she gives you any trouble, gag her." He fished in his pocket and produced a handkerchief. "This ought to do." He tossed it in Mr. Roth's direction.

Mr. Roth missed it and had to dive to the dusty floor to retrieve it. He straightened with a scowl, dusting it off on the leg of his pants.

Rose shuddered in revulsion at the thought of the filthy piece of cloth coming anywhere near her lips.

"Stop your sniveling, Mr. Roth." Blaine's voice was mocking as he pulled open the door. "This will all be over soon." He stepped outside, slamming the door behind him so loudly that both Rose and Mr. Roth winced.

Mr. Roth shifted awkwardly from one foot to the other, refusing to meet her eye.

"How could you?" she hissed. "My aunt trusted you. *I* trusted you!"

He wrung the handkerchief between his hands. "I'm sorry, Miss Rose. Truly sorry for my part in this."

"I can see that." His distress was palpable. "I don't know what hold that despicable man has over you; but whatever it is, I forgive you. Please. Just untie me, so we can alert the sheriff before Blaine harms anybody else."

Mr. Roth hung his head dejectedly. "I'm not at liberty to do that, Miss Rose."

"Of course, you are! You're at liberty to do whatever you wish!" She raked her gaze up and down his too-thin frame. His black suit hung loose on him, reminding her of a scarecrow. "You have two good hands and two good feet." What was wrong with him?

"It's not that simple, miss." He sounded genuinely regretful. "I have too many debts to pay and too many collectors nipping at my heels. If I don't receive my cut of the ransom money, and soon, I'm a dead man."

Understanding settled in Rose's gut, sickening her further. "You're a gambler," she accused in a dull voice, knowing with sudden certainty she wouldn't be getting any help from the likes of him. It made her sad to realize that he'd been playing a part the entire time he'd pretended to give her dance lessons. The only thing that didn't make sense was how thoroughly her aunt had been taken in by the antics of both men. Winifred Monroe wasn't one to extend her trust lightly, but at some point...

"I'll admit I've had my share of bad luck." Looking indignant, Mr. Roth drew himself up stiffly. "Things are about to change, though." He rubbed his hands together gleefully, as if already counting his share of the ransom money. "I'll be living the good life soon, far from this countrified speck of a town."

Rose stifled the urge to laugh in his face. He was both a

criminal and a coward. If he truly thought that either of those attributes was going to lead to any modicum of success, then he was also touched in the head. She rolled her shoulders to work out the knots in them and was shocked to feel the ropes holding her wrists loosen.

She wiggled her hands, and the ropes slid to the floor. They were free! For a moment, she was too shocked to do anything but wiggle her fingers experimentally.

From beneath her lashes, she darted a look at Mr. Roth to see if he'd noticed the ropes lying on the floor behind her chair. She discovered he was no longer paying one bit of attention to her. He was too busy pacing the warehouse, muttering to himself like a lunatic.

She flexed her ankles to gauge the strength of her other bonds. To her dismay, he'd done a better job of tying her legs than he had her hands. It was too bad. She glanced around her, looking for anything within reach that she might use to cut the ropes. Her movements caused the full skirt of her gown to shift sideways. She tried to straighten the skirt to cover her ankles once again, but it remained pulled to one side as if something heavy was holding it there.

It took another moment or two for her to realize that the item in question was resting in her very own pocket. *What in the—?*

Her thoughts raced over the way Lancaster had stumbled into her earlier, along with his cryptic insistence afterward that she recite her first lesson back to him. *He must have taken the opportunity to slip something inside my pocket.*

Which could only mean one thing. He'd been suspicious of Blaine's intentions from the start — probably of his intentions in behaving like something less than a gentleman after leaving the gunsmith's shop. If Lan had harbored any inkling that Blaine intended her actual harm, he would've never allowed her to leave the building with the man.

She darted another furtive glance in Mr. Roth's direction. He was still muttering to himself. His head was down, and his hands were shoved deep inside his pockets.

Lord, please keep him distracted for me. She slowly moved a hand out from behind her chair, inching her fingers toward her skirt pocket. Any sudden movements might draw her demented captor's attention to what she was about to do. To her enormous relief, her fingers closed around a small pistol. She didn't recognize its shape, so it probably wasn't one she'd shot before. However, Lancaster had taught her the fundamentals of how most guns worked. All she needed to do was remove the safety, aim it, cock it, and pull the trigger.

Every gun is loaded. Every gun is loaded. Please, God! Let this one actually be loaded with real bullets.

It had to be. Why else would Lan have gone to such trouble to slip it inside her pocket? He'd likely only been pretending to lose his balance. Arming her had been his sole purpose in pretending to stumble.

She held the gun behind her, keeping her shoulders rolled back as if her hands were still tied. Then she called across the room to Mr. Roth, "I say good riddance to both you and Mr. Eastman! My aunt can hire a new man of business, and you never were that impressive of a dance instructor in the first place. Neither of you will be missed."

Mr. Roth whirled in her direction, his pale face flushing with anger. He produced Blaine's handkerchief and waved it at her. "I'd advise you to keep quiet. Otherwise, I'll have no choice but to gag you like Blaine said."

"Oh, that's right." She feigned surprise. "You're one of

those sorry creatures who does exactly what he's told." She gave him a taunting grin, hoping to provoke him into moving in her direction. "Like a good hound."

His jaw worked with anger. "That's enough out of you, miss. I'm warning you!" He stomped closer.

"Or what?" She lifted her chin in challenge.

"Don't be a fool," he sneered. "In case you've forgotten, you're tied to a blasted chair."

She waited until he moved across the room to stand directly in front of her. "Am I?" She swung the pistol around with one hand to aim it directly at his chest.

His eyebrows shot so high into the air that she was amazed they didn't fall clean off. "How did you—?" He scrambled a few steps back, freezing when she cocked the pistol.

"Not another step, or I'll shoot." She reached down with her other hand and was amazed to discover the ropes at her ankles had been tied in a simple bow. With a snort of disbelief, she tugged them loose. "I was trained by one of the best gunslingers in the west, so I assure you I won't miss."

Rising to her feet, she spared the phony dance instructor a tight smile. "Blaine was correct when he called you a fool. Both of you are fools for thinking you could take on Winifred Monroe's niece and the love of Lancaster Tracy's life, while coming out ahead." Blaine could mock her humble beginnings all he wanted. She was proud of who she was and even prouder of who she'd become.

She stepped away from the chair, waving Mr. Roth toward it. "Sit!"

Trembling from head to toe, he complied.

"Now tie your feet to the chair, and you'd better do a better job of it than you did with mine. Or else," she threatened in a low, furious voice.

Mr. Roth was such a terrified ninny that she was no longer the least bit afraid of him. Her only concern was hurrying since Blaine could return at any moment. The instant Mr. Roth's feet were secured, she stepped behind his chair. "Stuff the handkerchief in your mouth and give me your hands." When he followed her orders as docilely as a lamb, it was all she could do to hold in a hysterical chuckle. She quickly tied and triple-knotted the ropes around his wrists. Not that she was overly concerned about how well they held. All she needed to do was slow him down long enough for her to escape from the warehouse.

She jogged across the room and cracked open the door. A hasty look in both directions proved the alley was empty of all creatures except for a thin, hungry-looking cat. "You poor thing," she murmured. "I'll come back with some food when this is over."

She stepped outside and sprinted up the alley with the gun held in front of her, slowing her pace only when she reached the corner of the building. Peeking in both directions, she took off again, jogging up a short hill toward the beginning of Main Street. She was both surprised and wildly relieved when Blaine did not reappear to stop her. Where was he?

Fear clogged her throat at the thought that he might be confronting her aunt this very moment, demanding and extorting money on her niece's behalf.

And he was armed!

Continuing on toward the boarding house, she was so intent on scanning the street in front of her for any sign of trouble that she stumbled over a pothole. Her ankle twisted painfully, nearly bringing her to her knees.

"Mercy!" White hot pain shot up her leg, telling her she'd sprained it. Or worse! By some miracle, she was able to keep walking on it, but just barely. She limped slowly towards the sheriff's office. "Please, God. Just get me a little farther." She continued to murmur prayers as she painstakingly hitched her way up the far end of Main Street.

A horse whinnied, making her halt in fear. She watched in silence, hardly daring to breathe, as a wagon rumbled over the next knoll and headed in her direction. Her shoulders slumped to see it was only Jensen holding the reins to a team of horses that looked as old and raggedy as himself.

He lifted his hand in a cheerful wave. However, his expression turned pasty with alarm at the sight of the gun in her hands.

"Is everything alright, Miss Rose?"

"No!" She glanced fearfully around them. "I was kidnapped and held for ransom, but I got away. Almost." She glanced ruefully down at her sprained ankle. "I tripped and injured myself. It's slowing me down."

"Whoa, there! Who-o-o-oa!" Jensen brought his team of horses to a halt. "How about I drive you the rest of the way to the sheriff's office, miss?" He leaped down from his seat, casting a worried glance at her ankle. "It'll be faster than walking."

"Hobbling, you mean." She shot him a teary smile full of gratitude.

But Jensen never got around to lifting her into the wagon seat beside him. Blaine darted from the alley to their left. He aimed his gun at the former livery owner as he crept closer to them. "Run along, old man. Rose and I have a personal matter to resolve. You'll only get in the way."

"We most certainly do not!" She couldn't believe how easily such bald-faced lies dripped from his traitorous tongue these days. "Shame on you for trying to fleece my aunt with your blasted ransom request, Blaine Eastman!"

She raised her revolver at him, preparing to fire it over his head in the hopes of scaring him off. "After all she's done for me, I'd rather die!"

"That can be arranged." Blaine bestowed a hard smile on her as he shifted his gun away from Jensen to train it on her. He moved around the side of the wagon to face her. "*After* the old bat pays handsomely for your safe return." His ugly smile indicated he had no intention of doing anything honorable by her afterward.

A fearful silence settled between them.

"I hope you're prepared to wait a very long time for that day, Mr. Eastman." Sheriff Branch Snyder's voice cut through the tension as he sat up in the back of Jensen's wagon.

Rose blinked in astonishment to realize he must have been hiding there throughout the entire encounter. His pistol was already outstretched, only inches from Blaine's temple. "You're going to have plenty of time behind bars to contemplate your sins. Let's see. There's kidnapping, blackmail... Oh, and embezzlement charges, according to the report Winifred Monroe filed in my office just this morning."

Blaine pivoted angrily in the sheriff's direction, still brandishing his weapon. However, he froze at the sound of yet another revolver being cocked.

"If you so much as hiccup, you're a dead man," the sheriff's newest deputy warned, sitting up in Jensen's wagon beside his boss. "We do, however, appreciate that tidy little confession of yours in the presence of so many witnesses. Makes the paperwork that much easier."

"Blaine Eastman," the sheriff intoned, producing a set of handcuffs as he leaped over the side of the wagon, "you're under arrest for kidnapping, blackmail, and embezzlement.

Go on and lay that weapon of yours on the ground, nice and slow!"

Jensen winked at Rose, who was close to collapsing. "Sorry for all the theatrics, miss." He stepped closer to her. "But it was necessary to get a proper confession. You're safe now." The old cowboy slung a surprisingly strong arm around her shoulders and hoisted her at long last onto the wagon seat.

During their short ride to the sheriff's office, Branch Snyder commenced his official interrogation of the glowering Blaine Eastman.

Jensen continued his gleeful explanation in undertones to Rose. "When Mr. Tracy caught sight of Mr. Eastman so soon after he was supposed to be escorting you to the dressmaker's shop, he figured something had to be wrong. He checked in with your aunt to be sure and discovered you'd never made it home. The two of them went straight to the sheriff's office to report you missing." He angled his head in disgust at the man in handcuffs behind them. "And apparently to file charges of embezzlement. If you ask me, jail is way too good for that bloke!"

Chapter 8: Corrected Assumptions
Rose

Rose followed the sheriff and his deputy inside the sheriff's office to give her statement. Branch Snyder took one look at her ankle and hastily invited her to sit on a chair beside his desk. Throughout the interview, she relaxed in slow degrees. It felt so good to know she was safe again. By the conclusion of their interview, though, she was trembling from head to toe.

"What's wrong with me?" She held her arms out in front of her, alarmed to find out she was powerless to hold them still.

"You've been through a lot, Miss Addington." Sheriff Snyder moved across the room to pour her a cup of coffee. "Here you go, ma'am." He returned to her and set it on the desk beside her, tossing a harried look toward the front door. "Be assured, I've already sent word to your aunt. She and Rupert will be on their way soon to take you home."

"Thank you, sir." Rose's thoughts flew to Lancaster. Where was he? She could only imagine how frantic her disappearance had rendered him. Knowing him, he was probably kicking himself up one side and down the other.

"My pleasure." The sheriff gave her a sympathetic smile as he hitched a hip on the edge of his desk. "You'll be pleased to know Mr. Roth was waiting in the warehouse right where you left him."

Her lips twitched despite her trembling. "Tied up, you mean?"

"And blubbering like an infant." He chuckled without mirth. "I've never seen anything like it. He couldn't rat out Mr. Eastman fast enough to the deputy who went to collect him. Apparently, he's more afraid of the loan sharks catching up with him than going to jail." He shook his head. "An all-around pitiful fellow."

The door to the sheriff's office flew open. "Rose," her aunt called brokenly. "Oh, my dearest niece!" Instead of Rupert, however, Lancaster was the man rolling her wheelchair into the room.

Rose's gaze locked with his. "Aunt Win," she breathed. "Thank heavens you're alright!" She struggled to stand, wincing as her weight landed on her injured ankle. In the end, all she could do was stretch her arms out. She was forced to wait while Lan strode in her direction.

Aunt Win watched in rapt fascination as he swept her niece into his arms. He cuddled Rose against his chest, twirling her around several times.

She reached up to thread a hand through the hair waving against the back of his neck, pressing her face against his neck.

He muttered huskily in her ear, "I heard you found my gift."

"I did. Thank you." She raised her head to reverently touch his cheek, monumentally grateful they were still alive. Never before had the sight of him been so welcome. So precious. Her trembling subsided at the knowledge that her prayers had been answered. Everyone she loved and cared about was safe again.

"I'm glad." His eyes were suspiciously bright.

She sensed he could still use some reassurance. "Things might not have turned out so well without your quick thinking." It no longer mattered to her that her aunt was witnessing her every move. She was head over heels in love with Lancaster Tracy. It was impossible to continue hiding it. Nor did she want to.

"Or your bravery." He turned his face to press a fervent kiss against her palm. "Even so, I may never forgive myself for allowing you to leave my shop alone with that animal."

"We didn't have any reason to suspect he was up to something so unconscionable," Rose protested. Her biggest fear at the time was that Blaine might renew his attempts at flirtation. Or press her for a firmer response to his request to escort her to the barn raising.

"But I did," her aunt confessed in a tone of deepest remorse. She rolled her wheelchair closer. "I've had a pair of detectives sniffing through my records for days to investigate my growing concerns in his direction. I should've said something to the sheriff sooner. This is my fault." She shook her head in despair at her niece.

"No. It's Mr. Eastman's fault," Rose corrected firmly. "He's the only one to blame here." She bit her lower lip to hold back a chuckle. "Though I'm happy to say he sorely miscalculated his prey when he went up against a woman courting a gunsmith."

Lancaster's arms tightened around her, making her wonder if he considered her statement to be a slip of the lip. "Oh, dear," she teased, catching his eye. "I reckon this means the cat is out of the bag about us!"

"Out of the bag and at least a half mile down the road,"

he agreed with a grin. He didn't look the least bit concerned by it.

"Oh, pshaw!" Her aunt slapped a hand through the air. "I might be getting up there in years, but I can still read. The first day we stepped inside Lancaster's shop, I saw the flyers about the shooting lessons he offers. Three short little lessons, not the dozens he showered on you. I suspected all along he was only using them as an excuse to court you." Her twinkling eyes took the sting out of her words.

Rupert hurried into the building and reached for the handles of her chair. More than likely, he'd lingered outside to tether the horses.

"Then you do not object?" Rose caught her breath at the realization she'd sorely underestimated her aunt. Again.

Aunt Winifred gave a dry cackle as she reached over her shoulder to pat one of Rupert's hands. "After I turned down Mr. Eastman's offer of marriage to you, he promptly turned around and kidnapped you. I don't want to even contemplate what a gunslinger of Mr. Tracy's caliber might do if I turn down his offer, as well."

Joy flooded Rose as her shocked gaze flew back to meet Lancaster's warm, assessing one. "You already asked for her blessing, didn't you?" Her heart raced like a stampede of wild horses while she waited for his answer.

"And she gave it, darling, like I promised you she would. The rest is up to you." He gently placed her back in the chair beside the sheriff's desk so he could take a knee in front of her. "Will you marry me, Rose?"

"Yes!" She didn't like the sight of her tall, strong gunsmith reduced to kneeling. "I love you so much," she whispered when he leaned forward to enclose her in his embrace once again.

"I love you more." Despite their audience, he brushed

his hard mouth against hers in a warm, tender promise. Then he stood, drawing her gently to her feet.

Branch Snyder leaped forward to clap Lancaster on the back. "Allow me to be the first to congratulate you!" He heartily shook their hands. "Please forgive my exuberance, but we don't get too many marriage proposals here at the sheriff's office." He shook his head, grinning. "In fact, I'm fairly certain you're the first."

He was still grinning when Rupert pulled open the door to wheel Winifred Monroe from the building. Lancaster proudly followed them with Rose in his arms. To her surprise, Rupert didn't hand her aunt into the carriage at the curb like he normally did. Instead, he assisted her into the driver's seat outside.

It was a kind gesture on both their parts, one that allowed Rose and Lancaster a modicum of privacy inside the carriage. But only a modicum. Her aunt waved at them from the open window between them and the driver's bench, clearly intending to remind them of her presence.

She didn't turn around until Rupert lifted the reins to get the horses trotting toward home.

Lancaster took advantage of their chaperon's lapse in attention to cuddle Rose closer. "It's a good thing you already agreed to marry me, because I have a confession of my own to make." He tightened his arm around her shoulders. "And no matter how irritated it makes you with your future husband, he's not letting you out of your promise to spend the rest of your life with him."

She drew back a few inches to scan the hard planes and angles of his face. "What are you talking about?" If he was trying to worry her, it wasn't working. She loved and trusted him too much.

He waggled his dark eyebrows at her. "I'm talking about

A Mountain Tryst by a certain *R. Addington.* After you left my shop yesterday, I noticed how close you were to finishing your manuscript, and I couldn't resist. I sat down and finished copying the few pages for you."

"Oh, Lan!" She threw her arms joyfully around his neck. "I love you so much that it hurts."

"I'm not finished." He brushed a kiss against her earlobe. "Before leaving the shop, I packaged up your manuscript, marched it down to the post office, and sent it off to that publisher in New York you've been yammering up a storm about."

Apprehension gripped her. "You did *what?*" She feared she'd heard him wrong. *Correction.* She most assuredly hoped that she had!

"Oh, for pity's sake, child, he submitted your manuscript to the biggest publisher in the country! He did you a favor." Her aunt's voice carried through the open window between them. "If you've been keeping any other secrets from me, dearest, now would be a lovely time to clear the air between us. How can I support your dreams and aspirations if I don't know the half of what's going on in your life?"

Rose tipped her head against Lancaster's shoulder with a moan of capitulation as Rupert steered the horses up the driveway leading to her aunt's palatial home. "I didn't think you would approve, Aunt Win, and I didn't wish to disappoint you. Not after all you've done for me."

"We're family now, Rose, and family sticks together." Her aunt's voice was thick with emotion.

Not always. Rose drew a sobbing breath. *My mother was proof enough of that.*

"What I meant to say," her aunt corrected sheepishly,

"is that *this* family sticks together. From now on," she added fiercely. "I'm not losing you again, dearest!"

Happy tears coursed down Rose's cheeks at what her aunt was offering — unconditional acceptance of everything that made her who she was. Her love for Lancaster Tracy. Her gift for writing. Possibly even her penchant for landing herself in scrapes, though she wasn't counting as much on her aunt's support of that last item.

"I thank you from the bottom of my heart." Rose sniffled damply. She planned to hang on just as tightly to her aunt. "I don't want to lose you, either!"

Aunt Winifred gave one of her delighted cackles as Rupert halted the carriage in front of the porch stairs. "While we're on the subject of confessions, I believe that beau of yours has a few more to make, but we'll leave the two of you alone for that."

While Rupert assisted her down from the carriage and gently lowered her into her wheelchair, Lancaster pushed open the carriage door and leaped to the ground. He reached back inside for Rose, who ended up in his arms yet again. He walked with her around the wide, covered veranda to the back of the house. They took a seat on a cushioned bench there, overlooking her aunt's prized rose garden.

As her gaze landed on the lush blooms, her thoughts were awash with hopes and dreams of the future — their future. Hers and Lan's. Together.

"Wild roses are my favorite flower." He raised her hand to his lips to kiss the front and back of it. "Ever since I met one particularly lovely Rose."

"I'm flattered," she confessed in a deceptively soft voice, "but not enough to let you out of sharing whatever final secrets my aunt alluded to."

He barked out a laugh. "You're very much Winifred Monroe's niece. I couldn't be more enchanted." Without warning, he swooped in for another kiss that left them both breathless.

"I'm still not letting you wiggle out of your confession," she murmured when he raised his head.

"Fair enough." He toyed with a strand of hair dangling against her cheek. "Since your aunt insists on blatant honesty, I reckon you have every right to know you're marrying a wealthy man."

Though she was surprised to hear it, she was far from appalled by the news. She wrinkled her nose at him. "There are worse things in the world, you know." She'd been picturing far more grizzly secrets, ones involving skeletons in closets and the like.

"I was born wealthy," he continued, "to a family in the hotel business back east."

"Oh?" That surprised her, especially coming from him — a man who'd spoken so disparagingly about her own quick acclimation to her aunt's luxurious lifestyle.

"Unfortunately, there were strings attached. Big, heavy strings. My family wished to control me. To mold me into a person I had no interest in becoming. They even picked out the woman I was to wed, someone I barely knew and did not love—"

Rose's gasp of alarm made him grin. "Here and I was wondering if I was ever going to get a rise out of you."

"You are mine, Lan. Mine and no one else's," she informed him fiercely.

"That I am, darling. That I am." He tucked another errant strand of hair behind her ear.

Knowing how independent his spirit was, her heart ached for the way his family had treated him. He must have felt like he was suffocating while attempting to grow into the man he was meant to be. She wrapped her arms around his middle. "I'm sorry to find out what you endured back home."

He hugged her tightly. "It was nothing compared to the hardships you suffered down south."

"I don't agree." She pressed her cheek to his chest. "We both suffered in our own way, but our collective suffering brought us to where we are today. Here. Together." She would endure it all over again if that was what it took to be with him.

"It did." He kissed the top of her head. "I want you to know that I willingly left it all behind — my family, my home, and my wealth. Though I have a trust fund in my name, I haven't touched it since the day I headed west. I worked my way here as a bounty hunter, sometimes with an empty belly while sleeping under the stars. I learned a lot, grew stronger on the inside and outside, and ended up settling in Cedar Falls. You know the rest of my story. You know what kind of man I've become. You know exactly who you're marrying."

"I do." She tipped her face up to his. "And I couldn't be happier about it." He'd forged his own path and made his own money. She slid her arms around his neck to pull him down for another kiss that he delivered wholeheartedly.

Looking back, it had been a long and twisted journey west, one fraught with many hardships. However, Rose had no regrets. Every sleepless night and every back-breaking day of work in the scorching summer heat had brought them one step closer to finding each other.

"You're my home now, Rose." Lancaster cupped her cheek in one large, callused hand.

"And you are mine," she whispered back.

They sat there, wrapped in each other's arms, while the breeze stirred the petals of the wild roses in front of them. Rose snuggled closer, secure in his love that she was confident would last through all their coming tomorrows.

Chapter 9: Wedding Bells
Rose

September

Lancaster hadn't been raised in church, nor had he ever considered himself to be a religious man. As his wedding day dawned, however, he was overcome with awe at the knowledge he would soon be wed to the woman of his dreams.

After donning the only suit he owned, he took a knee beside the bed in his cabin. He'd already promised to build Rose a bigger home — anything she wanted. In return, she'd assured him countless times that she would be perfectly happy living in his cozy mountain paradise.

"Thank you, Lord." Lancaster clasped his hands in front of him on the quilt that covered his mattress, wishing he could think of something more eloquent to say to the Maker of All Things. However, he'd always preferred direct speaking, and his gut told him that the good Lord could handle such.

"From this day forward, my life is Yours. My family. My

business. My home and everything in it." Children, he hoped, dashing the back of his hand across his eyes as he stood and reached for his hat.

He'd rented a buggy for two from the livery so he could drive his bride home in style after their wedding. It was already hitched up outside. He pulled open the door and stepped out onto the porch, pulling the brim of his Stetson down against the morning sun.

The hay fields around him were ripe and ready for the final harvest of the season. Afterward, Cedar Falls was preparing for another barn raising. This time, at his homestead. He'd offered to pay the townsfolk for their trouble, but they'd insisted on everyone pitching in like they always did.

You're one of us now, they'd said, though they'd assured him he was more than welcome to foot the bill for the feast that would follow. He was more than happy to do so.

Jogging down the porch stairs, he untethered the team of horses and leaped into his rented buggy. The trip to the church didn't take long. It was punctuated here and there by distant claps of thunder. A few harried glances at the sky didn't show a cloud in sight, though. Probably no more than an electrical storm. This part of Texas was famous for them.

Since Lancaster was nearly an hour early, he was surprised by how many wagons were parked outside the church when he arrived.

Rose's aunt met him in the foyer, perched in her wheelchair like a queen on her throne. She was wearing a new silk gown of autumn gold, and her hair was piled in a complicated twist on top of her head.

"There you are, gunslinger!" She held out both heavily be-ringed hands to him.

He hurried forward to lift them to his lips. "How is she this morning?"

Winifred Monroe didn't have to ask who he was referring to. "Our sweet summer Rose couldn't sleep a wink last night. Her heart was too full over the prospect of becoming your bride today."

"When may I see her?" he asked quickly.

"As soon as you hightail it down to the altar." Her aunt wagged a bony finger at him. "You'd best get moving since the wedding is about to begin."

He frowned in confusion at her. "I thought it wasn't scheduled to begin for another—"

"There's a storm on its way, son." She waved him toward the sanctuary like he was no more than a pesky fly. "The minister promised to begin the moment both you and my precious niece are ready."

"I'm ready," he assured, striding through the sanctuary doors and down the aisle to take his place at the front of the church. *More than ready.* It felt like he'd been waiting his entire life for this day.

The church pianist launched into the opening notes of the bridal march. Rose appeared in the back of the sanctuary on none other than Jensen's arm. It was fitting that she'd asked the older fellow to do the honors, since he was the one who'd first driven her into town, right past the doorstep of Lancaster's gun shop.

Jensen's gaze glinted with emotion as he led Rose in Lancaster's direction. He looked proud enough to bust the buttons clean off his suit jacket.

Lancaster's gaze shifted to his bride-to-be, and everyone else in the room disappeared. Her blue-green eyes glowed into his. The happiness spilling from their depths was even more beautiful than the white satin dress she was wearing. She looked like an angel, floating his way in it.

They reached Lancaster's side. Jensen removed her hand from his arm and placed it on Lancaster's. "God bless you both," he said gruffly. Then he turned around to take his place in the front row beside her aunt.

Lancaster laid his other hand protectively over Rose's, and they faced the minister together. The ceremony was short and simple, just like they'd requested. However, it was no less eloquent because of its brevity. Their vows were equally short and to the point, requiring nothing more than a simple *I do* from both of them.

The minister closed the ceremony with prayer and pronounced them man and wife.

"I love you, Mrs. Tracy." Lancaster didn't hesitate to seal their vows with a kiss that left no doubt in anyone's mind that he was desperately and irrevocably in love with his bride.

"I love you, too, Lan." Joy spilled through her smile and rang in her soft, musical voice. They turned together to face those who'd gathered to celebrate the momentous occasion.

They were ready to begin the newest chapter of their lives within the cozy hideaway of Cedar Falls.

Thank you for reading
Wild Rose Summer!

Ready to read about the next tall, rugged, and swoony cowboy bachelor who moves to Cedar Falls?

Pick up book #6 in the

Wild Rose Summer

Brides of Cedar Falls Series.
Going All In

A cozy historical romance filled with a Texas Ranger's hilariously awkward attempts to win the heart of his mail-order bride!

Sneak Preview: Going All In

A *Texas Ranger who wants a wife, an heiress who needs a husband, and a marriage of convenience that sparks an accidental attraction in this sweetly suspenseful and squeaky-clean historical romance.*

Despite a dangerous and demanding career, Texas Ranger Bolt Sanderson dreams of starting a family. But a man who spends most of his time on the road doesn't exactly have a long list of marital prospects. He decides to cut a corner on his quest for happily-ever-after by firing off an application for a mail-order bride.

Scarlett Martinez must be married for an entire month before she can claim her inheritance, but a disastrous first social season has her spiraling toward spinsterhood. She runs across an advertisement for a mail-order bride and realizes she's found the perfect loophole...until her cowboy lawman groom swaggers to the altar. Their unexpected attraction — and the danger that accompanies it — is a complication neither of them was counting on.

Grab your copy of **Going All In** *in ebook, paperback, or Kindle Unlimited!*

Sneak Preview: Hot-Tempered Hannah

Book #1 in the Mail Order Brides Rescue Series

A bounty hunter is on the trail of a missing mail-order bride who looks identical to the only woman he's ever loved.

When Gabe Donovan is recruited to track down a missing mail-order bride, he receives the shock of his life. She could pass as a twin to the partner he thought he lost in a fire — the same woman he never got around to confessing his feelings to, for fear of ruining their partnership. If she's still alive, she must have faked her own death. Leaving him precious little time to track her down before the past she's been running from finally catches up to her, and he loses her again...this time for good!

Pick up your copy in ebook, paperback, or Kindle Unlimited to start reading this complete 12-book, sweet historical series!

Mail Order Brides Rescue Series, book #1: Hot-Tempered Hannah

Get A Free Book!

Join my mailing list to be the first to know about new releases, free books, special discount prices, Bonus Epilogues, and giveaways.

https://BookHip.com/LSPKMHZ

Sneak Peek: Cowboy for Annabelle

Annabelle

To dodge a group of ruthless debt collectors, an impoverished southern belle agrees to become the mail-order bride of a rugged cowboy in this sweet and uplifting historical romance!

After refusing to marry the cruel new owner of her childhood home, Annabelle Lane finds herself on the run from the scoundrels he hires to change her mind. In desperation, she signs a mail-order bride contract and hops on the next train, praying the groom she is matched with is a man worth running toward.

The most sought-after range rider in the west, Ethan Vasquez is highly skilled at protecting livestock from bears, wolves, and rustlers. But it's a job that leaves no time for courting, no matter how determined he is to have a family of his own someday. When a dare from friends has him scrambling to send off for a mail-order bride, he never imagines how quickly she will arrive or how much trouble will follow. It's a good thing he knows a thing or two about handling predators. He can only hope she finds his heavily scarred hands worth joining with hers in holy matrimony after the first wave of danger is past.

Start reading
Cowboy for Annabelle.

This trilogy is available in eBook and paperback on Amazon + FREE in Kindle Unlimited!

Sneak Peek: Bride for the Innkeeper

January, 1892 — Albuquerque, New Mexico

Lacey Cleveland pulled up the hood of her cloak. She remained in the shadows of the alley between two clapboard buildings as she adjusted the precious bundle against her shoulder. Her tiny nephew was fast asleep beneath a faded patchwork quilt, the last memento she had of her late sister who'd been a magician with a needle and thread. For the thousandth time, she experienced an enormous sense of gratitude that the toddler was still so young. By the grace of God, the eleven-month-old would remain oblivious to the many troubles they were facing, the least of which was their desperate need to flee from New Mexico.

I will keep us safe from him, little one, if it's the last thing I do. With one last furtive glance down the alley to ensure they weren't being followed, she finally stepped into the full blast of morning sunlight. It was early, barely eight o'clock. She planned on being the first customer to darken the door of the mail-order bride agency in Albuquerque.

Though her knees trembled with apprehension, she walked without looking to the right or the left. It was an old trick her gypsy parents had taught her. *May they rest in peace.* When a person held their head high and moved with purpose, they were less likely to be questioned. Or beheld with suspicion. Or even noticed, for that matter.

Out of the corner of her eye, she watched a farmer rattle past on the cobblestone street with his wagon full of milk jugs. Though he tipped his hat in her general direction, she could tell he was paying her no real mind.

Another block of walking brought her to her destination. She slowed her steps at the sight of the cheerful sign, freshly painted white letters on a dark blue background. *Albuquerque Mail-Order Bride Agency.* Good gracious, but her life had sunk to a new low at the necessity of darkening the door of such an outlandish establishment! *Forgive me, Lord, for what I am about to do.* Answering the advert felt all too much like selling herself on an auction block, but she was fresh out of better ideas. If marrying a perfect stranger was what it took to get her and her nephew safely out of town, then she was willing.

"May I help you, ma'am?" A matronly looking woman, wearing a somber high-neck gown of green wool, was seated behind an antique cherry wood desk. She glanced over the tops of her spectacles, eyeing Lacey from her simple up-do to her dusty boots.

"Yes, please." The thready sound of Lacey's voice wasn't the least bit contrived. She felt close to fainting as she breathlessly rattled off her carefully rehearsed speech. "My family suffered a terrible tragedy, which left me alone in the world with no money and a little one to raise on my own. I can see no other recourse but to marry with haste." It was the closest explanation she could give to the truth without outright lying.

To her relief, the woman's severe expression relaxed at the mention of the babe in her arms. Her thin lips wavered into a faint smile as she rose. "Have a seat, please." She waved one angular hand at the cozy overstuffed chair parked in front of her desk. "I'll fetch some refreshments."

Over the course of the next hour, Lacey was fed, counseled on the merits of signing a mail-order bride contract, and successfully bound by her signature to marry a man by the name of Edward Remington.

"He's an innkeeper in a town bearing the lovely name of Christmas Mountain," the woman sighed. "Doesn't it sound like something straight from a storybook?"

It did, but life had taught Lacey that looks and sounds could be frightfully deceiving. The fact remained, she was about to become wed to a man she'd never met, a man she could only hope would treat her and her nephew better than her jailbird of a brother-in-law.

"Are you certain he will not balk at the notion of me arriving with a babe in my arms?" Her thoughts swam dizzily as she pondered the possibility that Mr. Remington might have no interest in becoming a father, at least not so soon.

The matchmaker shrugged. "He did not rule out the possibility of marrying a widow, though our application most certainly gave him the option."

Lacey caught her breath, wondering if she should set the woman straight on her marital status. She'd not been previously wed, much less widowed. After an inner debate, however, she decided it was wiser to let the woman assume her husband was deceased. Disclosing that her brother-in-law was behind bars might increase the chances of her whereabouts being reported back to him.

"How soon may I wed this Mr. Remington?" she inquired nervously.

"I can have you on the mid-morning train, if you wish." The woman smiled in understanding. "Mr. Remington has provided a generous allowance for your travels. Enough, I dare say, to provide for the sustenance of both you and your babe."

Lacey momentarily closed her eyes against the sting of grateful tears. "How can I ever thank you?" she whispered.

"By becoming the best innkeeper's wife in the west," the woman retorted, leaning forward in her chair to sort through the required paperwork. "Arranging another successful marriage will bolster our company's reputation, as well as our profits."

The best innkeeper's wife in the west? Oh, my! It was a tall order, indeed. A wry chuckle chased away Lacey's tears. Until now, she'd been so focused on survival that she'd not given a single thought about whether her groom would find her suitable for *his* needs.

Good gracious! If she was being perfectly honest with herself, she didn't know the first thing about running an inn. A wave of uncertainty swept over her as she pondered the many things she would undoubtedly have to learn. Even so, a clean, well-run inn sounded like the perfect place to raise a child. He would have a roof over his head and plenty of food in his belly.

Shaking off the tendrils of self-doubt, Lacey lifted her chin and met the matchmaker's gaze. "I would be delighted to catch that mid-morning train."

Jo Grafford, writing as Jovie Grace

Start reading
Bride for the Innkeeper
today!
The Mail Order Brides of Christmas Mountain trilogy is available in eBook, paperback, and Kindle Unlimited on Amazon.

About the Author

Jovie Grace is an Amazon bestselling author of sweet and inspirational historical romance books full of faith, hope, love, and cowboys. She also writes sweet contemporary romance as Jo Grafford.

1.) Follow on Amazon!
https://www.amazon.com/author/joviegrace

2.) Join Cuppa Jo Readers!
https://www.facebook.com/groups/CuppaJoReaders

3.) Follow on Bookbub!
https://www.bookbub.com/authors/jovie-grace

4.) Follow on Facebook!
https://www.facebook.com/JovieGraceBooks

Acknowledgments

A huge, heartfelt thank you to my editor, Cathleen Weaver, Karen Edwards, and my sweet beta readers for sharing their thoughts and feedback on this story. I am also wildly grateful to my Cuppa Jo Readers on Facebook for reading and loving my books!

Jovie's Titles

Brides of Cedar Falls

Lawfully Witnessed

Wanted Bounty Hunter

The Bounty Hunter's Sister

Rescuing the Blacksmith

Wild Rose Summer

Going All In

Mail Order Brides on the Run Series

Cowboy for Annabelle

Cowboy for Penelope

Cowboy for Eliza Jane

Mail Order Brides of Christmas Mountain Series

Bride for the Innkeeper

Bride for the Deputy

Bride for the Tribal Chief

Mail Order Brides Rescue Series

Hot-Tempered Hannah

Cold-Feet Callie

Fiery Felicity

Misunderstood Meg

Dare-Devil Daisy

For a printable list of my books:

Tap here

or go to:

https://www.jografford.com/joviegracebooks

For a printable list of my Jo Grafford books

(*sweet contemporary books*)

Tap here

or go to:

https://www.JoGrafford.com/books

Made in the USA
Middletown, DE
01 September 2024